Published by Forever Inspired Publishing

# ELDERS FOR GUIDANCE, YOUNG MEN FOR WAR

## Acknowledgements

This is a long time coming. I remember as a kid watching my favorite cartoons on Saturday daydreaming about me crafting my own superhero story. Something that was birthed from my mind alone. To see that finally come to fruition is a literal dream come true. This is the first of many Creations of mine and trust me, there's so much more to come!

Foremost, I'd like to thank my mother, Mrs. Barbara 'Ms. Bee' Tucker! She's always been in my corner from the beginning; believing in me and my writing when no one else did.

I want to say thank you to my family and friends that have also seen something major in me.

My editor and manager, Tamara Hamilton, you took a chance on me, my stories, my life. You saw something great in me and I'm forever grateful for that and I appreciate you so much!

I hope you as the reader enjoy the peek into my mind. It might seem a little hectic in here but have a seat I think you're going to love the show! Enjoy the first of many books to come.

Welcome to my world,

DLT.

# ELDERS FOR GUIDANCE,

# YOUNG MEN FOR WAR

## BY: D'ANGELO TUCKER

# Chapter 1

Deep in the southern most parts of the United States of America, Antebellum 1846

Tobacco leaves are ripe and ready for harvest, anchored to their thick stalks hanging motionless under the blazing hot summer sun awaiting the weather worn and beaten hands of chattel slaves to pluck them from their post and shove them into burlap sacks. Sacks that once they are weighed will be sent off to the factories for processing. The proceeds from those leaves and the free labor that acquired them all goes back to the owner of those slaves and of that plantation.

A hard day's work should yield each individual 100 pounds a piece of raw product. Anything less will be met with harsh punishments ranging from whip lashings to days in the box. A 3 feet by 3 feet rectangular vertical holding cell constructed of solid iron. Unbearably uncomfortable in either the summer or the winter months.

The Missus of the house had come to rest on a rocking lounge chair facing the main tobacco fields where she took up delight in watching her families throng of black slaves diligently picking and packing away the cash crop that built their families wealth and made their names prestigious among their peers. The missus children play games of chase and ring around the rosie in the front yard not too far from where she sits.

Off in the distance her husband and his farm hands drag an adolescent black girl kicking and screaming to a wooden post in the center of the courtyard where they have tied her hands to a metal stud protruding from the top of the beam. Her feet kicked aimlessly searching for something solid beneath them. She was panicky and drenched in sweat. The summer heat bared down on her already exhausted body. The master of the house spoke to the overseer in low tones as they glanced over at the young girl. She pleaded with the men not to harm her but her pleading was to no avail. The Master was handed a rough brown cow skinned leather whip that he unraveled slowly, building up the anxiety in the young girl intentionally. The frayed tip of the whip fell to the dirt generating a small wisp of brown air that lingered. Her begging intensified as her cries transformed into the sounds of anguish as the brown leather bit into her brown flesh peeling back tissue revealing the soft pinkish red beneath. Ten lashes and she had passed out from the pain and trauma. She was lowered from where she'd been

2

suspended and her limp body was handed off to one of the elders of the slave camp who immediately began rendering aid to the poor soul.

The Master took a handkerchief from his back pocket, swiping the navy blue cloth across his sweaty brow and the nape of his neck. He handed the whip off to his overseer as he headed back up to the big house to get himself a refreshment after a long day's work of chastising his workers. To him those slaves were no better than his mules used to plow the fields . A whip drove them to work their hardest as well but unlike those slaves the animals understood what constituted a whipping and therefore they would work until they died. In his opinion his slaves were lazy and therefore required greater motivation. The Master's wife met him at the steps of their mansion holding a glass of frigid lemonade that dripped condensation on her pristine hands, hands so soft and unmarred. Hands that have never seen a day or even an hour of rigorous labor and according to her husband's wishes, she never would. He smiled and kissed her on one of those hands then on her lips before taking the cold beverage.

From one of the slave quarters an elderly woman with a haze of white film covering her pupils scowled at the mansion adjacent from the quarters.

Her mouth was tight lipped as she glared at her master drinking and reveling in the conversation he carried with his wife. Seething hatred for them both boiled deep in her heart like an overflowing cauldron. Behind her the other elders worked on the young girl, first cleaning the wounds with water and witch hazel, meant to cleanse and reduce swelling and infection. Next, they added salve as a protective measure, a barrier that will allow the wounds to properly heal. That young girl writhing in pain was the elder woman's granddaughter. Her daughter had been sold off by the master many summers ago in exchange for a new plow and mules for the field and the elder assumed parental responsibilities. The elder muttered some curses under her breath.

Later that evening as the sun was setting, a servant from the house wandered over to the slave quarters with instructions from the master. It was his children's bedtime, and the normal routine was a bedtime story narrated by the young girl that he whipped previously that day but seeing as she would be down for a few days he needed someone else capable of storytelling to report to the big house. It was the elderly woman that eagerly volunteered. The years of abuse and hard labor bore down on her tired flesh and bones as she shuffled methodically towards the grand structure lit up with what seemed like a thousand candles. Candles were posted in windowsills and suspended from gold laden ornate chandeliers that hung from the ceilings of almost every room in the house. House servants stood at attention in every doorway awaiting orders from the residents.

A servant led the elder up a winding flight of stairs towards the west wing of the house where the youngest of the master's offspring slept, two children a year apart, a boy and a girl. The presence of the elderly woman startled them at first. They were expecting the young vibrant black girl that they were used to. The Master's daughter asked about the young black girl's whereabouts but her question was answered by her brother who knew exactly what had happened to her. There was almost an undertone of pride in his voice when he spoke as he explained to his sister what had happened to their normal storyteller and why. The elder woman in that moment wanted nothing more than to claw his little demonic face off but an act like that would spell out danger for her and the other slaves as there was much to do and see in the coming future. So instead, she bit back those emotions and forced a smile to take shape on her full worn lips. She was guided to a seat where she snuggled in taking in the momentary rest off of her feet and exhaling a grateful breath. She whispered a prayer to herself then gazed around the beautifully decorated room taking in all of the wonderful sights surrounding her.

"I thought you were blind."

One of the kids asked. The elder turned her head towards them with the same forced smile plastered on her face.

"Child, you don't need eyes to see what you can see and what you can't see. Yall so use to seeing what's in front of ya that you can't see what's ahead of ya."

That statement confused the children. The little girl fiddled with a stitched doll nervously as she studied the creepy woman's face.

"You're supposed to tell us a bedtime story?", the young girl questioned reluctantly.

The elder nodded and sat back in her chair.

"What kind of story I be telling, you chirren? You want fantasy, you want fairytales, or you be wanting something more...special."

Both children shouted simultaneously that they wanted the special story.

"Alright, lay back and I'll tells ya a good time story. It's about magic. It's about good and evil. This is the story about the Black Phantasm. Y'all ever heard about the Black Phantasm? Oh, he's a powerful something. They say his coming is marked with gray skies and the gathering of a whole heap of ravens and black birds. And the smell of death, um hmm. Some say he's a man, others say he something else. Lay back chirren, Ol Mama Odu gots a good one for you tonight."

As Mama Odu spoke the children sank deeper beneath the covers like their soft cotton stuffed beds were suddenly transformed into pits of quicksand. Fear coiled up their spines like a cold wind in the dead of winter and nestled in their little black hearts.

# Chapter 2

Days later as the sun crests over the horizon, the wind kicks up to a sturdy gust causing the wind chimes on the porch to sing their songs. The iron weathervanes shifted left to right in the increasing breeze as dark clouds rolled in overhead. A slave child lingering near Mama Odu's shack brought attention to the changing weather.

"Yes child, the weather changing and bringing something on its currents. Y'all come on in here and sat down now and let God do his work," she says as she gently nudges the child to the shanty.

Hunting dogs packed in kennels whine and pace the limited space as if they could detect that something more than a storm was coming. The overseer stood beside the Master helping guide his horse to the stable when he took notice of the change in weather as well. Tipping his mangy hat back as he peered into the gray void above with a puzzled look on his face.

"Looks like a storm's rolling in…"

The master also looked up at the darling skies with little worry upon his face. "A storm was nothing new in these parts at this time of year so no cause for concern." He kicked the overseer in the shoulder from atop his nag, tearing the field hands' attention away from the skies and back to his duties.

A little while later as the Missus lay on her lounge chair in the living room facing large bay windows that looked out over the plantation, one of the white field hands in charge came bursting through the front door yammering about pesky ravens gathering on the fence line near the roadway and how he would kill them all before he let one of those rats with wings destroy the Misters crops. The field hand went to the armory and retrieved a long rifle and a handful of rounds and marched back outside with a determined stride. Minutes later rifle reports were heard echoing across the plantation as the murder of crows perched on the wooden fence post scattered in all directions. The wind steadily picking up as the day progressed on and with that the current brought a putrid smell.

When night came the creatures inhabiting the forest held off on their nightly chorus, instead the forest fell silent as if instructed to by some supernatural presence. The overseer stepped out of his quarters when he noticed the silence. With a torch in hand, he peered out into the darkness as far as his sight would allow surveying the plantation as an eerie feeling washed over him. The feeling that he was being watched. He decided the weather was the contributor and shook it off. He spun on his heels slamming the heavy wooden door behind him with a hollow thud. A black form emerged from the shadows soundlessly as it swept from one side of the structure to the other, the resident inside unaware they were being observed.

The overseer settled in at a tiny, squared dinner table in the center of the shack to feast on a bowl of assorted meat stew with vegetables and almost fresh bread. As the first spoon full of stew was approaching his hungry lips, a loud sound just beyond his meager kitchen window arrested his attention. Upset that someone would have the audacity to interrupt his meal he pushed himself away from the table with an angry grunt and snatched up a plank of wood in his hand as he stomped towards the door.

Twisting the handle while yanking the door back exposed him to a strong gust of wind and two nostrils full of that putrid smell that loitered all day which made him wince. After a brief investigation around his shack, he was satisfied that it had to have been one of master's pets roaming the plantation searching for a meal of its own and he turned to head back indoors. He was violently met with a long razor sharp dagger that pierced the back of his head where the spine merged with the skull. The blade slid through his medulla oblongata with little resistance and into the soft gray matter of the brain, completely shutting down the man's motor functions, his screams ceased before they ever left his mouth.

He was rolled over onto his back where he couldn't feel the blade bite into his chest but he could hear the sound of bones cracking and saw droplets of blood dot the tip of his nose and cheeks. The last thing he remembered seeing before he succumbed to darkness was the shadowy figure wrenching out his still beating heart and discarding it to the side like food waste. As the overseer drifted off to the endless sleep of death, he watched the intruder sprint off in the direction of the mansion of his sleeping master, helpless to warn them of the pending doom.

A guard sat slumped over in a chair on the front porch of the mansion. A jug of 80 proof moonshine lay tipped over near his feet encompassing the man in an aura of potent potato brewed liquor. He snored loudly as the drink held him under the spell the spirits had cast. He was unaware of the intruder stalking up the porch stairs and didn't feel his life drain from his body through the new slits on either side of his neck severing the carotid arteries. His hat was then pulled down over his face and from a distance it appeared he was fast asleep. The dark figure moved about from room to room unnoticed by the slumbering occupants, the bottom of his fur moccasins absorbing the impact of his footsteps.

      The master's son lay asleep in his bed until the sharp creaking of a door opening stirred him awake. His room was cloaked in darkness, all but the moonlight that trickled in through the bedroom window providing just enough light to make the outline of things visible to his waking eyes and play tricks on them. The door to his room was wide open but the doorway was filled with a void of darkness seemingly darker than the night skies beyond his bedroom window. Something in the young boy surged forward brought on by fear, fear of the unknown. Fear that something in the void was staring back at him. After some time his quickened heart pace slowed back down to normal beats. He was about to shut his eyes when a large, gloved hand slipped out of the darkness and gripped onto the edge of the door pulling back and closing it shut. The young boy sprung up in his bed with a renewed fear taking hold of him. A layer of ice cold sweat coating his body caused the blonde hairs on his neck and forearms to stand on end. The boy mustered the strength and willed himself out of bed, tiptoeing to the door. His little head poked out of the room and jutted back and forth expecting to see some nightmarish creature lurking around the bend and peeking around the corner at him with glowing red eyes that could set your soul on fire but there was nothing. The house was still. Too still. No servants were standing on hand. No guards milling about. The boy followed his instincts which led him up the stairs to his parents' room but when he arrived the door was ajar. As he shoved the door back, the sight filled him with horror. His mother and father lay massacred upon their bed. Pools of blood soaked the mattress and sheets and some spilled over the edge staining the floor. His own screams first filled his head then the space around him as he took in the scene. Someone or something has brutally murdered both of his parents.

Just then a sound coming from the bottom of the stairs captured him. There was a crackling then, a sound unmistakable to an outdoorsman. The soft orange glow that grew in size followed by deep black smoke confirmed the child's suspicions. Fire! He raced back to the top of the stairway and glanced down through the billowing saber colored smoke. Through the flames the young boy spotted the silhouette of a man standing in the front doorway motionless. The man wore a dark bandana around his face obscuring his features but those eyes although human they held something else, something sinister. Something akin to the idea of the creatures lurking in the dark parts of the boy's mind.

As smoke permeated the house the other children awoke to the calamity unfolding and soon discovered they were trapped by the raging inferno. Screaming and coughing as the poisonous gas invaded their pure lungs robbing them of precious oxygen, the children beat on their bedroom doors until their cries fell silent.


At the slave quarters Mama Udo awoke to the sounds emanating from the big house across the field. The orange glow of fire illuminated the slave shacks pushing back the night. When Mama Odu stepped out into the courtyard she drank in the sight and smiled with delight.

The Mansion was a blaze from floor to rooftop, every room burning with an unstoppable fury, a sight she prayed earnestly for many years. The heat from the fire was immense and she could feel the warmth on her skin from that great of a distance. She closed her eyes and raised her hands toward the sky in a measure of praise for the random turn of events. One slave turned to look at the overseer's quarters and they all gasped at the sight of him dead, mouth agape and his rib cage burst open in a bloody mess.

A man, cloaked in shadow, stood in the fields between the slave quarters and the mansion. The flames provided more than enough light to outline key details on the figure. He in fact was a man. He wore dark clothes and the cloth that concealed his identity. A belt and gun were holstered on his waist; the belt was dotted with spare rounds that glimmered like bits of gold against the fires light. Another belt and holstered gun lay strapped over his chest, and a long rifle was slung over his shoulder. He held a long bloody knife in one hand. Mama Odu cautiously approached the man until she was within arm's length. They stared at one another silently, understanding what each one was saying to the other. A single tear welled up and streamed down her wrinkled almond toned cheek. It wasn't tears of sorrow but of joy because she knew what this was, what it meant. The mysterious figure nodded to her and she nodded back in concordance. Then she turned to the crowd of stunned slaves who watched the fires raging and addressed them.

"Hear me now. You's all free as of tonight! You's free! Grab up what belongings you need. Weapons and tools and you and ya kin flee to them woods! Heads north until you reach freedom town and don't you stop for nothing but to rest! Never return to this place! It's cursed ground! Now GO!"

She waved her hand seemingly snapping the mass out of the hypnotic trance that fire can put someone in. As they dispersed to do as she commanded, she turned back to thank the masked man but realized she was standing in the field alone. She smiled again before turning back to her people preparing for the journey.

# Chapter 3

Modern day

Langley Air Force Base- Hampton, Virginia 2041
Subterranean Testing Facility Location 002

A balding gentleman wearing a white lab coat and holding a tablet stood in front of five well-built men in tan shirts, camo jeans and boots. The room they stood in was disgustingly generic with white walls, white tile floors and ceiling. Nothing of great importance stood out or any details indicating where they were exactly in the building. Nothing other than the number 4 in big bold red print on the outside of the door. Behind them a host of other doctors and scientists donning the same lab coats were busy preparing vials, needles, and double-checking equipment.

"Good evening gentlemen and thank you for your attendance. I am Doctor Donald Stansfield; lead researcher and I head up the Research & Development departmental wing of this facility. Myself and my staff develop new cutting edge technologies for the future. Some of our projects are in-house while others are sourced out work directed from this government, governments abroad, and various military industrial complexes, within our country's alliances, of course. You all hail from different military or combat backgrounds and because of that you all were selected by your respective commanding officers for your particular sets of skills. You will undergo a brief physical and psychiatric evaluation beforehand then we will move on. My assistants will handle the initial procedures. Please go with them."

The five men turned about face in unison and followed a young lady out into the hall which was as whitewashed and generic as the room they'd just exited. The hallway was long and narrow, barely accommodating two people walking shoulder to shoulder. There was a series of numbered doors as well as far as they could see before the hallway bent sharply to the left.

"Airman Marion Marks, please follow me."

One of the assistants said as she held out her hand towards room number 10. The door was opened and inside were medical equipment and a large chair like the kind you would see in a hospital. The assistant ushered Marion to sit, and she began preparing equipment.

Marion Marks. Air Force Airman, Pararescue. He was a tall dark skin black male, athletically muscular with cunning eyes. He bore a series of tattoos that riddled his body from head to toe, some were art inspired while others were nearly a means to cover or distract from the ugly scars of battle branded into his skin but all of them were positioned tastefully to where when he wore his Class A uniform all the body art was concealed. The assistant placed sensors on his fingertips and a blood pressure band around his hulking bicep taking notice of the large hammer like illustration with bird wings and muscular arms holding a black rifle etched on his forearm. Marion recognized her intrigue, and it was as if he read her mind.

"It's the insignia for my squadron. Air Force PJ's 720th Special Tactics Group. The Spec Ops community said we were some heavy hitters, so they started calling us falling hammers. Because to a hammer..."

"Everything else looks like nails."

Even though the assistant wore a medical mask Marion could see the smile behind the cover as the corners of her eyes creased. She finished her portion of work and led Marion back to waiting room

19

Four. He was poked and prodded two dozen more times before chow time. While the men quietly consumed their meals, Dr. Stanfield entered the cafeteria.

"Good evening gentlemen, please excuse my interruption and please continue eating. I'm sure you are all famished after today's physicals. I have collected all of your data profiles, and everything checks out green. We can proceed with training in the morning. I'll leave you all to your devices. Good night gentlemen."

The doctor departed without saying another word.

The next morning at 0600 hours the men were roused from their beds and marched back to room four.

"Yes, good morning, good morning gentlemen, I take it you all had a pleasant night's rest. If you will, please follow me."

In the coming days the men had been through a rigorous test of physical endurance from miles ran on the treadmill to live fire shooting scenarios in a controlled shoot house. These military men checked out as the doctor had expected. As they sat in a holding room for a brief pause in testing the men spoke among each other. Questioning why they were there. Complaining about the constant poking and prodding that's been going on, more so than what they endured going through MEP's at the beginning of their military careers.

"I feel like a gotdamn pin cushion."

"Is anybody here gonna ever tell us just what the hell is going on or are we just gonna sit here looking like jack asses?"

On the third day their wishes were granted. After testing Dr. Stansfield joined them in the holding room. He brought with him a laptop that he unfolded when he sat down at a desk near the front of the room.

"It has been brought to my attention that some of you have wavering confidence in the reasoning why you are here. You were all selected for mission specific requirements. You were all assigned to a clandestine program. The project's code name is Chronostream.

"Chronos like Zeus's father, the Father of Time?"

"Precisely, time. Time is a finicky construct.  And it is the most valuable possession we can never renew or obtain in this lifetime. The only resource in this entire existence that we cannot regain once lost . Until now."

The room fell silent as the doctor spoke.

"Science recently has achieved a tremendous breakthrough that will revolutionize history and mankind's contributions to it as we know it. With Project Chronostream the exercise of utilizing a piece of prototype hardware designed by Darpa and coupled with our research. We've created a time displacement technology that theoretically allows the wearer of the device the ability to slip in and out of the Chronostream at any particular point through the methods of destabilizing the wearer on a molecular level converting that energy into digital form for easier access into the stream. The most suitable way to traverse the stream and reconstitute the individual once they've reached the desired location, point, and time .

"Slip in and out of the Chronostream at any point in time. Doc, are you telling us that you have a time machine at this facility? That your team actually cracked the code that dozens of scholars, hell the great Einstein couldn't even crack?"

The doc stirred in his chair, quietly contemplating his response before answering.

"Yes Lieutenant, well something of that nature. The technology is complicated but, in a nutshell, yes. "

The room erupted in conversations. The idea of time travel has been a popular concept for decades bordering on centuries, but no one ever thought it would be an achievable goal in our lifetime. But there they were, sitting in a subsection testing facility at a U.S Air Force Base involved in a D.O.D lead project involving theoretical time travel. The doctor corralled the men's attention once again. Reminding the men of the NDA they signed at the beginning of trials.

"Well, is it safe Doc?"

The doctor shifted in his seat.

"Relatively, yes. We had 82% success rate in solid material time displacement transferal with the previous model of the skiffs we utilized for testing.

We expect that percentage to have increased to 96% with this latest model."

"Skiffs?"

The good doctor nodded, removing a small handheld device from his lab coat and holding it up for the room to see. He demonstrated how the device looked by sliding his hand into the finger hold and securing it with bands around the wrist. The device resembles a dark metallic mesh glove with intricate circuits and a large touchpad on the top of the hand.

"This is a Skiff, in accordance with the Chronostream and the theme of sea travel. Think of the expansion of time as a river and the current is the ripples of time and everything that occurs in one's own individual time stream. Well currents flow generally in one direction as time is perceived to. Now, similar to a current, a worthy sea vessel can traverse that stream either with or against that current. With the Skiff the user can input a specific location, date, and time onto the device and travel the stream to that particular point in the stream."

"And how is this even possible?" asked another Lieutenant.

"TMDFR. Temporal Molecular Deceleration and Full Recombination."

Some of the men protested the methods the doctor and his staff chose to input living specimens into the stream. These men weren't molecular biologists by any means, but the idea of molecular deceleration just didn't sit well with them. The whole while they complained and debated the safety aspects of the program Marion Marks sat quietly in his chair contemplatin'. Out of everyone in attendance he was sure he had lost someone more valuable to him than anyone else here in their lifetime. His loss was much more devastating. Thalia was her name, and she was his wife once upon a time. She was the peace in his chaotic world. He lost her while he was on deployment in the Middle East. She was brutally murdered by an intruder during a home invasion one unforgettable evening. He didn't even receive word of her death until days later and it crushed him. Marion was lost and the only way he could bring himself back was to find something solid to anchor himself to or the misery of her death and the depression that kept him company would consume him. And no one was the wiser until weeks later when his neighbors complained to the housing authorities about the rancid odors creeping from under his front door. To avoid a bullet in the head Marion chose better and decided to pour himself into his work as a poor attempt to defuse the heartaches, volunteering for deployments in some of the most hostile terrain. Some would say he had a death wish and he did but all of his psychiatric evaluations, checked out.

Dr. Stansfield was giving these men a chance at making history but more than that, this was potentially going to give Marion a chance to see his beautiful wife even if it's only one more time. To him the reward outweighed the risk and for someone with nothing to lose, that was reason enough, he was sold on the concept. He slammed his hand palm down on the plastic table abruptly ending all surrounding conversations.

"Doctor Stansfield, could these trials aid in a permanent means of time travel for all of us? I don't know anyone else's situations or losses and to what magnitude but if you're telling me there's a chance no matter the danger or how minimal the probability that I could see lost loved ones again I'm in!"

Dr. Stansfield stared at Marion for a moment taking in his statements then glanced around the room. When no one objected, the Doctor closed his laptop and pulled out his cellphone, placing a call.

"Prepare the skiffs for test trials. The men are ready, thank you."

# Chapter 4

The men were fitted with their skiffs and the trials went underway. The first test was to see how the men fared with the deceleration, so a short test was performed.

"You all will be traveling back in time 1 minute to this exact location. The timer will begin and at 0 you will be returned to the present moment."

The countdown commenced. There was static at first then a flurry of lights and distorted images as their bodies were deconstructed and sent up stream. Then just like that the men were back in the laboratory only they were standing a few feet behind themselves. The sounds around them were slightly muted and there was a bit of haze over their view, but they were back in time one minute. They were shocked and amazed! Dr. Stansfield and his teams truly conquered time travel and these brave men were the first to experience it, truly a historical moment indeed.

They watched as their future selves completed the skiffs safety checks and the countdown followed. They watched as their bodies dematerialized right before their eyes. The signals on the skiffs flashed orange alerting the men that the sequence was preparing to start again. Static, lights, distorted images and they were back in their original timeline. The men were gasping like they just ran a mile and sweating profusely but in one piece.

"Well, gentleman? How was your trip?"

The Doctor's response was a chorus of wide grins and laughter at the fact they'd just done the impossible. The staff immediately began recording health data and downloading the onboard A.I. systems stored on their chest rigs. The first jump seemingly was a success.

"Gentleman, congratulations you're the first in history to successfully time travel. That will be all for today, rest up. My staff will be monitoring you closely for the next 48 hours before the next stream jump. Good evening gentlemen."

Dr. Stansfield patted them all on the back as he exited the labs cheerful of this momentous accomplishment. Later on that evening Marion checked his watch, a habitual activity that spawned from his days in active duty status, constantly checking time and coordinates before, during and after deployments. He read the time on his watch then the time on the digital clock attached in the corner of the lounge area. The two times were off by 11 minutes. That was odd. This couldn't be possible. The time trials took him back 1 minute exactly that's what the assistant said and what he witnessed. They returned directly to the current present time. So how was his watch time off by so much? The idea grasped a hold of his mind for hours finally he willed his brain to put the endless array of theories to bed deciding this is definitely a thing he would address to Dr. Stansfield at the next visit.

Days later as the team reviewed data and prepared for the next time trial an IT specialist was reviewing energy output readings when he noticed a series of spikes and valleys occurring during the time displacement with 2 of the 5 Skiffs. The tech brought the issue to his supervisor who also reviewed the data.

"The energy spikes appear during the Molecular Transference phase. The Skiffs require a considerable amount of electromagnetic energy to separate the atoms on a molecular level. The human body is a conduit for electromagnetic energy. The interference could be a direct result of the earth's own naturally occurring magnetic polarity during deceleration. Boost the positive ionic charge output and that should stabilize the peaks and valleys."

The tech did as he was instructed, and it leveled out the energy output immediately. The days passed and the work went on and the team presented test after test, building up the lengths of each time jump. On this particular day, the team was suiting up for the biggest jump to date. Going back two days' time. The scientist and techs had generated several new modifications to the skiffs and jump gear as results of the live testing. They'd gained knowledge in areas that they hadn't even explored before and achieved new strides in the evolution of technology capabilities needed.

The team wore a high durability flexible organic metalloid nanotechnological fiber woven bodysuit the same materials used to house the Skiffs technology. The suits allowed the wearer's molecules to bond with the metalloid fibers during molecular declaration to become more fluid while in the Chronostream. Think of it the same way a life preserver vest inflates during water submergence. That buoyancy accelerates ascension through the Chronostream. The metalloid fibers operate in the same fashion when exiting the stream allowing for a swifter recombination. The Skiff energy output

31

readings were stable but teetering. Dr. Stansfield notated this and deemed the levels safe enough to proceed. The time coordinates were imputed into the Skiffs and the countdown began.

The loud animated voice counted down the seconds till Skiff activation but seconds before they activated, Marion's Skiff had a catastrophic malfunction resulting in a severe energy spike output that scrambled the operating functions of the time piece. By the time the technicians were alerted to the energy spike the shift occurred.

They tried to emergency abort the mission, but Marion's Skiff activated. He phased out in a violent burst of static electromagnetic energy that bowed out in all directions blowing out the semiconductors connected to the facility's generators along with every other electrical device within a 300-yard radius.  The pulse temporarily knocked everyone caught in the blast unconscious, laying immobile on the floor of the lab.

Dr. Stansfield's ears rang, and his head pounded when he regained consciousness and began standing up. There was a revolting taste of burned metal that lingered in the back of his throat frying his sinuses and jostling his brain. When his hearing returned, his earbuds were being assaulted by the wailing of claxons as amber colored lights flashed. His assistant was stirring awake at the same time he was.

"Dr. What...what happened?" the assistant asked shakenly.

Dr. Stansfield looked around at the other facility workers scrabbling to find hand holds or to even gain their balance while others rushed to silence the alarms.

"Doctor Stansfield." One technician addressed the lab doctor.
"The backup generators should be coming online any moment now."

"Please, gather your wits about you. I need to assess the situation and I'm going to need your assistance."

As the Doctor stated this, the backup generators kicked in and power was restored to the facility. The techs began rebooting their computers bringing everything back online. The assistant commanded control of the main monitor and after inputting command prompts was brought to a data screen.

"Bringing up Skiff number 4's tracking beacon locator now. Oh, oh my God! Doctor .... DOCTOR STANSFIELD .. You want to come and see this!"

The doctor rushed to the console and what he read he couldn't believe. The Skiff locator beacon read its current position was 200 years in the past. Santee, South Carolina.

Dumbfounded by both the fact the technology works and that feeling in the pit of your stomach when you know something has gone terribly wrong. A realization of a black man with Marion's high intellect and combat effectiveness in the American South in 1841.

"Get the other Skiffs back operational! This is no longer a test; this has become a rescue mission. We have no idea what condition Mr. Marks is in, but I fear the worst. Every second, every minute, that he remains in that location of the stream could be days, weeks, or even years for him in our timeline!"

Santee, South Carolina 1841

Marion lay naked motionless in a bushel of tall reed grass near the bank of a gentle swaying

34

river. The warm water lapping up against the southern mud banks had a rhythmic droning that slowly awakened him. The beating sun burns hot on his bare skin as he returns to his senses. The sweet smell of honey suckles mixed in with the tangy scent of swamp mud mingled in his sense of smell and there was something else. The scent of burnt wires. Looking down at his hand at the Skiff, is when he realized it was destroyed somehow and now rendered useless.

Also, he noticed he was stark naked head to toe. Where'd his suit go but more importantly where was he? When was he? Images flashed in his mind, and they must've been the moments he passed through the Chronostream. Something had gone wrong and he felt it. He felt different. He couldn't explain why he just knew something had gone wrong and the Skiff was damaged beyond repair. Until he could find the facility there was nothing, he could do about it. Marion pushed himself to his feet and looked around for any signs of life but all that he could see was swamp lands for miles in every direction.

"Fuck...."

He began pushing his way through the thick brush and swampy terrain. It was a challenging task between the biting flying insects, the thick sludgy swamp mud and the host of lethal creatures lurking just below the water's murky depths. He sloshed through the wet terrain for what felt like forever until he eventually came to a clearing where a dirt road ran through it. Sounds off in the distance caught his ear and instinctively he took to the brush for hiding as he waited to observe what type of vehicle approached but more than that were these hostiles or friendly.

A run down jack legged workhorse attached to a rickety wooden wagon decorated with several rusted metal bands meant to hold the slacks together clinked dully against one another as the wagon rolled along. It was occupied by three filthy looking white men, two rode the bench seat in the front and the third, a portly man, sat hunched over in the flatbed spilling corn whiskey all over his chest as the wagon's misshapen wheels hobbled over the ruddy dirt road. Painted on the side of the wagon in cherry red paint read 'Billiards Farm'. Marion was puzzled about the way the men were dressed. He trumped up their means of travel to convenience and country life. Still, a naked black man suddenly appearing from the bush wouldn't be embraced so well by anybody so he decided not to reveal himself and instead waited for them to pass. He trailed the roadway sticking close to the wood when he came up on a house. There was a white woman hanging linen and clothes on various clothes hangers. Some of the items looked to be his size. The decision only took a millisecond.

Later, Marion was back hidden in the woods trying to figure out where he was. Everything looks aged but he could tell by the people and the language that he was still in the U.S just when? His thoughts were interrupted by a rumbling in the pit of his stomach and suddenly he couldn't remember the last time he ate or drank anything. And then there's the skiff, busted and seemingly useless for now with no way to troubleshoot it. This was turning out to be a long day for Mr. Marks.

Langley Air Force Base, Hampton, VA - Present Day

Dr Stansfield sat in the chair behind his desk tapping a pen rapidly on the desktop as if he were typing out morse code. The screen on his computer was lit up with the endless combinations of outcomes that resulted in the Skiffs catastrophic failure. The doctor was informed an hour ago that the skiff's Chronolocation blinked out, meaning tracking the subject was no longer an option. He and his team knew the last location of Mr. Marks but his condition or if he's even alive is a mystery to all of them still. His assistant's voice pierced the deafening silence brow beating him.

"Doctor, we've assembled the team and they are ready to jump, your presence is required in the laboratory."

In the lab Dr. Stansfield's address was brief and to the point.

"Airman Marion Marks, a part of this team, has been hurled through time and space. Tragically, his skiff malfunctioned, and we know the cause but not the effects. However, again, this is not a test trial it has become a rescue mission. Airman Marks Chronolcation's last ping was Antebellum South Carolina, 1841. Now, a Black man in that time period is complicated to say the least. We do not know his health condition but understand this is time, a period of history that actually existed, so we must be delicate on how situations are handled. The tiniest infraction could reroute American history or even world history for that matter. Please be gentle with your actions and needed adjustments. Good luck and Godspeed."

The techs prepared the rest of the Airmen for the time jump. The energy readings were adjusted and once they were maintained the jump sequence was initiated. In seconds another whole team was hurled through the fabric of time and space marked by the electromagnetic bubble that formed and dispersed leaving nothing in the space where the men once stood.

# Chapter 5

South Carolina, 1843

Dogs barked ferociously as they darted through the thick brush on the trail of a runner's scent. Behind those barking dogs were men. White men with guns and torches that illuminated the night as they stuck close to the blood thirsty hounds.

The runner was Marion who heaved heavy breaths as his mind raced. The night sky added little aid to his escape, for a normal man this would have been a run in futility. Airman Marks, though, was versed in navigation both with and without equipment. The shining North Star presented an invisible compass leading him through the muddy unknown. The dog's barking drew closer as he sloshed through the muck. Somehow the men pursuing him flanked him and were now tightening the noose. Outmanned and outgunned they finally cornered him near a hollowed tree. Marion understood war tactics and being behind enemy lines meant one of two things. Surrender and formulate a plan of escape later or die in the field.

He raised his hands in an attempt to negotiate his surrender when the lead hunter stepped forward and struck Marion across the temple with the redwood handle of his Remington 45 pistol. The unexpected blow stunned Marion and dropped him to a knee. And as Marion's mind spun and his vision blurred, he made out the barrel of the pistol aimed at him. Before he could think the assaulter pulled the trigger. The flash filled his sight. The percussion rocked his ear drums as the solid led slug slammed into his forehead...

The blast echoes in Marion's mind, jolting him awake as he sprang up from his sleep.

Lynchburg Virginia, 1856

That dream, that incident, replays in his mind every night since that night he found out just how serious things were. That's when he gained a deeper understanding of just how fucked he was. And how it somehow morphed into a blessing as well. That bullet that was fired with the intent of taking his life actually was his rebirth. It's staggering to the human mind when you discover that not only are you in a foreign time alone but you now have an uncanny ability. To his limited understanding, somehow the metallic organic flex suit that he

41

donned on the day he was yanked through the jump changed his own molecular structure, during the deceleration and recombination cycle. Some unseen mishap caused the metallic suit to reverse inward, coating his molecules and lining his flesh and bone with the material that was almost indestructible. That bullet did little more than dazed him and caused teeth-clenching pain but revealed his new superhero level ability.

It was early in the A.M. The time wasn't exact to him but the crickets were still chirping and the leaves were wet with morning dew so it wasn't dawn yet. The small campfire he started hours ago still flickered small flames that licked at the edge of the firepit. Marion slept with a pistol in one hand, always ready for conflict, a condition brought on by his current environment. Fifteen years has refined the special forces operator in him; sharpening that edge of his lethality. Primitive tools in comparison to what he was used to but when in Rome.

In the time since the jump, Marion has made a name for himself. The locals speak of him as a nuisance, but the Black slaves created Lore about him. They call him 'The Black Phantasm'. They think he's the spirit of vengeance for the past injustices done to blacks. And he'd been living up to the name. He started off with the killing of that hunting party that introduced him to his newer self.

After that, the misery he felt at another set of enormous losses sent him spiraling into depression. At rock bottom your real true self is revealed to you. At that moment an idea was born in his mind. His skills in this time period would put him ahead of the curve. He is virtually light years ahead of the most efficient soldier doing this time. He'd put these skills to good use and save those facing the same perils as him. It started as a crusade but over the years transformed into a movement. Now he's the most wanted man in the South. An ever-growing bounty on his head as the days rolled past. There are benefits that come with being impervious.

As Marion hunted for his breakfast though the dense Virginian forest, he found himself face to face with a black bear. Now, he did not wish to end this beautiful, majestic creature's existence but he must've stumbled into something because that bear was reluctant, and hell bent on ending his.

"Hey, buddy. I'm just out here looking for a meal just like you. Now hold up, I can't be your breakfast though."

The wooly beast roared loudly in response. Exhaling puffs of hot breath that looked like steam.

The animal drew closer, swatting at the air and slamming his massive paws on the dirt. Marion stepped back but the bear continued its path towards him.

"Ok Smokey, you want to dance with Poppa Bear, let's go then."

Both beasts roared as they charged into one another clashing hard and blending the lines where flesh meets fur, claws meet steel. A deep and hollow wailing echoed across the valley, indistinctive if the sound generated from man or beast.

A little while later Marion emerged from the forest covered in blood from head to toe. He dragged behind him all 300 pounds of the now deceased black bear. He dropped the body near the edge of a freshwater river where he removed his soiled clothes and entered the body of water in dire need of a bath. The icy waters rushed over his body washing away the crimson in gentle wakes of red that slowly diluted the bold color. There wasn't a scratch on him, not a drop of blood drawn was his. Being trapped in the 1800's as a black man was no walk in the park but the accident granted him the gift of being Impervious to physical damage, to what degree wasn't yet determined but as of right now he could add bear attacks to the list of things he survived. It came in handy. After field dressing the large mammal and relinquishing it of its glorious coat of fur. During the scuffle the bear's sharp claws slashed his shirt into ribbons that lazily draped off his physique. Luckily, he had a spare shirt in his bag but the mountains of Lynchburg gets uncomfortably cold at night around this time of year so the bear pelt actually turned out to be a God sent. Marion sat bundled up in it close to the campfire as the flames roasted the bear meat. He slowly rotated the meat on a wooden spit until it sizzled, and the edges were crisp and cooked to perfection. Afterwards he set the rest of the meat out to smoke near the smoldering embers as he tended to the maintenance of his tools and weapons. Cleaning every crease and crevice of his dual Colt 45 pistols. Brushing the large bore, freeing the weapons of any debris or build up and then he performed the same task on his long octagon bore .64 caliber revolving rifle that he added some modifications to. Some metal work and a telescopic looking glass made a decent mid- to long range sight that held its zero pretty well under fire, being what it was.

Once those chores were completed, he removed a map from the top pocket of his bag and unfolded it. It was a regional map that covered the states from the tip of Florida up to Delaware in intricate details. There were dozens of red circles dotting the states spanning from South Carolina up to the Virginia state line. The circles in the Carolinas were X'ed out. From where he sat now tucked away in a cove in the Afton Mountains, it was a two-day walk to the town's limit. He would either find what he's been looking for or he would add another X mark to his map.

# Chapter 6

Days later....

Lynchburg, Virginia

Lynchburg was a bustling town ever growing by the day. A ferry system started by the town's founder summoned tourists and travelers from all walks of life and the end result made this a very popular destination. A city worker was busy hanging posters in the town square. The posters were "Wanted" signs that read '$10,000 for any information that leads to the capture or killing of the Black Phantasm'. Below was a picture of a faceless figure with little to no details describing the suspect.

Across the walk a prominent figure in the town, Mr. John L. Levy stood outside of the swinging double doors of the Beaver Dam Tavern. The local watering hole and makeshift meeting place for the shot callers in the town. Mr. Levy scowled at the city worker as he went about his business posting the signs on every pole, the sheriff's office, and stage station. Mr. Levy's friend stepped out of the tavern and followed his eyes to see what he was gawking at.

"John, come on friend. I know you're not concerned about that nigger folk lore are ya?"

Mr. Levy scoffed as he turned to enter the tavern.

They found their seats at a round wooden table that has seen better days. The men parked near the rear of the establishment where tall mugs of foamy golden beers awaited them along with two other men that accompanied them. Cigar smoke drifted off beer battered breath as the local musicians played a tune on the upright organ and harmonica.

One of the two spoke.
"You know what I heard the Tanners plantation in Elizabeth City went up in flames not too far back. Heard the Tanners were never found and the property was burned to ashes."

"Yea I heard the same thing. My wife's friend was telling her that her family's farm suffered the same fate. The owner's whole entire family's gone. The house, gone. He owned slaves too. Said they saw signs them coloreds fled into the woods. I'm telling ya I never heard nothing like it." said Levy's friend.

Another man was about to lend the stories he heard about the Black Phantasm when they were rudely interrupted by Mr.Levy.

"Gentlemen, we're some of the most prestigious, well respected, wealthiest men in this town. My plantations almost tripled in profits in the last year. Carl, you're running the ferry service and its obvious that's bustling and Steven, your family came into all that land west of the mountains. We have bigger fish to fry than worry about some nigger lore and besides no one even has proof this Black Phantasm even exist. I refuse to occupy my intellect with stories that have no sequential meaning."

The men laughed as Mr. Levy made his argument. To them the notion did seem silly. They were happy someone was rationalizing their fears that were keeping them up at night.

"Twiddling your thumbs like nervously little schoolgirls about a ghost." said Mr. Levy shaking his head in disgust.

They were unaware that a surly man dressed in dark dusty clothes sat at the end of the bar in ear shot of them. He said nothing for a while and just listened as he sipped his beer wiping the froth from his lips with the back of his sleeve. It wasn't until the men began to make jokes about the topic that he became visibly frustrated and then emphatically he slammed the thick empty mug on the wood bar top with a loud slap that instantly silenced the crowd. As all eyes fell onto the man, he pulled a long cigarette from his pocket and struck a match on his thumb. The drag he pulled in was deep and lengthy. The smoke seeping from his nostrils and mouth seemed to go on endlessly.

"While you fine men laugh about that nigger lore, I have a story of my own I'd like to share with ya. Started 12 years ago. I too once was a prominent landowner. Had a wife, three children. About 50 slaves of my own working my fields day in and day out. I worked them got damn blackies for everything they was worth. Me and my family were happy. Until one day I came up on some men who were traveling salesmen. They specialized in discount niggers. Something wrong with them in one way or another but they were good for the money spent. Cheap labor so I bought the nigger for dirt cheap. They said he was a tough one to break but he was a sturdy some bitch. Had strange pictures etched in his skin. Intelligent too, for a nigger of course. I take pride in my knowledge of breaking a nigger, so I bought his ass. I tell you what, the first time I whipped him I whipped him good. I was panting like a damn dog in heat and he didn't bare any marks on one inch of his body. Puzzled the hell out of me but I had other methods. That ol turtle back eventually followed the rules and the routine. Even found himself a woman. Had a kid too. And that's what I wanted. A man that doesn't fear death, you can't harm him. But a man that has someone he loves means he has something to lose and well, he'll bow down to the devil himself to keep what he loves safe."

The stranger took another drag off his cigarette, tapping off a large gray portion of ash and continued his story.

"One day, that nigger got the bright idea that he, his woman and child needed to be free. Like I didn't pay my good hard earned money for them. They tried to run, got pretty far too. But I tracked 'em down. Shot 'em point blank in the head and left his ass for dead floating in a swamp bog. Drug his woman and child back to the plantation kicking and screaming. His woman wasn't as tough as him. She didn't last long.
Well, I thought that somabitch had sunk to the bottom of the swamp or something might've gotten

51

a hold of him and made him supper in them swamps and I'd never see him again but I couldn't have been more wrong in my life. He returned that night. Killed my wife. My children. My brother who stayed in the barn. Set my house a blaze. Some bitch almost took me out too, drove a blade in me just shy of my heart and left me for dead. I healed physically for the most part but my mind…my mind never recovered. I was lost. I'd lost everything and I had no hope. Then I heard about a plantation north of my own that had the same thing happen to them. Then I heard about another plantation and another. Then I realized it was him. Well, I swore my life to the cause that I'd hunt that dog down and send him back to the pits of hell with these two hands of mine."

One of Mr. Levy's friends looked around the bar at the patrons glued to their chairs as this stranger told his tale. Assuming it was a joke of some kind he spoke up.

"C'mon friend, you're telling us you saw this Black Phantasm? And lived? That ain't this man's way of doing things. I think you should be ashamed of lying to these people about a serious matter and getting them all worked up over nothing!"

The stranger spun so fast in his chair that it wobbled on three legs before toppling over. The tavern patrons could not have been prepared for what they saw next as the stranger ripped open the chest portion of his shirt exposing bare skin. A puffy pink scar ran vertically over sunburned flesh, almost dead center of his left lung. There was a maze of hard sinew like tissue crisscrossing his chest and up his neck covering a third of his face. Burn scars. The sight of his scars was horrific. The people in attendance gasped in unison.

"Does this change ya mind bout my story now, mister?"

The continued silence was his confirmation that they no longer took his story as just a tall tale. A young black girl sat quietly in the corner with her head down. She was one of Mr. Levy's slaves, particularly the one he preferred to travel with due to her usefulness inside and outside of the bedroom. Her clothes weren't top tier but a better quality than the average slaves. The bonnet she wore was oversized and concealed most of her face but she was gorgeous. An even toned perfect shade of brown, soft features and long thick sun-bleached locks that coiled under her bonnet. Her most stunning attribute though was her eyes.

53

Emerald green and her left one specifically held a unique feature. A mutation in her genetics caused a collection of gray pigmentation that formed into a triangle. She kept her head down not just because that's what blacks were expected to do but also because that stranger with the terrible scars was familiar to her even though she couldn't explain how or why.

Something about his presence sent chills coursing through her. She maintained her stillness even when the stranger stomped past her as he left the tavern. Soon the conversations reignited, and the music began to play again as if the stranger had never existed to them all but Mr. Levy who was consumed by the stranger and his story secretly because he worried about his own neck. The Black Phantasm could be a lore and nothing more. But that doesn't explain the rash of fires and murders dotting the coastal states. A smart man sees the enemy on the horizon and prepares for war rather than to excuse the potential threat. And with that he stood up and followed the man outside, his slave girl hopping to her feet and chasing behind.

Mr. Levy caught the man as he scaled the steps of his uncovered wagon. "Sir, these people are good people. Hard workers. God fearing, but they are soft. They are not used to the thoughts of war, the sight of death and brutal acts like such things that led to your physical condition. I do not believe in this supernatural entity, this Black Phantasm, however what I do believe in is what I can see, perceive with my own eyes. And I see something coming if it hasn't already arrived."

"Mister, trust you me. The calamity is already here. It just hasn't manifested itself yet. But I will tell you this if that black demon crosses my path again this time it's gonna be him that has the face off with death."

"You say this man was impervious to damage. So how do you presume you will accomplish this impossible task?"

The stranger said nothing, he just turned to the bed of his wagon and ripped back the thick black fabric covering. Beneath was an array of weapons the likes John Levy has never seen. Multi barreled rifles, things that resembled cannons but on a much smaller scale. And last but not least, jars of a clear liquid that shimmered in the midday sun. The jars bore the same explosive symbols as crates of dynamite. Either this man was crazy as a jack rabbit in heat or determined.

"What did you say your name was again, sir?"

"Dunner, Morgan Dunner."

"John L. Levy. Where would a man find you if a man was inclined to employ your services?"

"I'm staying in the brothel for now till I hear something about the next attack. You can find me there till then."

Mr. Levy nodded and shook his hand. He stepped back and watched as Dunner's wagon rode off trailing dust behind, a devilish grin plastered on his face.

# Chapter 7

Back at the Levy's plantation it was close to supper time. The table was set and the food was served. Every dinner seemingly went the same way no matter the number of people in attendance. It was always treated as a lavish event. A few servants stood quietly in their positions awaiting orders from the family and guests as they dined.

The number of random chatter filled the air along with the clicking of silverware on porcelain. To think, people that can live the horrid lifestyles that these folks live still find things to laugh and smile about. That always baffles the servants. During dinner hours the majority of the house staff were remanded to their quarters where they dined as well. Of course, the quality of food wasn't near the standards of the master and his guest's fare.

The slaves spoke in low tones, laughing silently and constantly being told or gestured to cover their mouths. Needing to hush up before the master heard them making all that noise. The occasional giggle would slip out between tightly pressed lips and bloated cheeks that struggled to hold in the laughter. The topic of the Black Phantasm wasn't lost to them either. The servants discussed the hopes and possibility that that entity did exist. Some made jokes of how they wouldn't lift a finger to save the master or his wretched children. One slave feigned as if he were the master's wife running into the Phantasm and being slaughtered. The death scene was so overly dramatic it caused an eruption of laughter that caused one of the seasoned mammy slaves to peek her head in the room and chastise the group for their noisy antics. Everyone chuckled and joined in except that young girl that accompanied the master earlier that day. Her name was Kyra but the other servants called her Berry. A name that followed her as a baby due to a strawberry shaped birthmark on her lower back. An orphaned child at the age of two, who was adopted by the slaves in the plantation where she was born.

According to her adoptive parents, her mother and father were killed and after their deaths the slaves fled the plantation during a fire. Months later the group would be captured by slave patrols and sold to auctioneers. Kyra and her new parents were bought by the Levys and she's been their property ever since. Too much of Mr. Dunner's story resonated with her and she could not explain why but she also couldn't shake the feeling that she knew him somehow. Even though she'd never met the man a day in her life. What she did know was that she did not like the feeling she felt being around him and she would rather never be around him again.

Santee, South Carolina 1841

The warm evening air crackled like the split end of a live electrical line. A spectacle of supercharged atoms ignite into a central point of energy no bigger than a pin top at first but then it expanded in size rapidly before the plasmatic orb distorts in an energy pulse that scatters in all directions causing the nearby wildlife to scatter , bending the swamp reeds and shuffling leaves and grass. In its place stood four humans, alien to this region with their full body suits, odd-shaped goggles and futuristic weapons and equipment. The men took up defensive positions as they surveyed their surroundings. The lead tapped a wrist mounted computer.

"Home base, this is the swimmers team. Jump was successful. Assessing jump location and then executing first part of rescue plan. Will report any updates as follows. S1, out."

"Swimmers, check and recheck gear before we move out. S2 and S3 establish a perimeter. S4, initiate Chronolocator confirmation. Let's find our man and get out of here before we fuck something up. The doc said we need to leave as little a footprint on this time period as possible and frankly the thought of putting a bullet in one of these back water fucks makes my dick hard so lets get on the move and get outta here. Hoorah."

The men set out on their task. Swimmer Four approached Lead Swimmer One.

"Sir, I checked the Chronolocators final ping and something's off. The time stamp was for 1841 and Mark's skiff malfunctioned 4 hours ago, present time. But my readings compared to his skiffs locator beacon are displaying that the skiff time frame is off, by a lot. Mark has been vacant in our time stream for a short period but in this time stream he's been here for 15 years...."

"Jesus, 15 years! He could be anywhere or long since checked out." S1 exclaimed while rubbing his forehead.

"Hey wait, I got something, I scanned news articles and mentions from this time stream, searching for anomalies, you know anything out of the ordinary. Two years prior was the start of a rash of plantation owners murders that spanned from South Carolina up the coast to Virginia. Each case is similar. The owners are killed along with the entire family. The properties were set on fire along with the crops. Any slaves aside from the overseer were freed."

"Scorched earth tactic?"

"Possible. That concept didn't come about till nearly the start of the second world war in 1937 almost a 100 years later."

"Sounds like our guy to me. Got damn! Military strong!"

"When do the fires stop?" asked S1.

"There aren't any more stories reported after the fall of 1856. Lynchburg, Virginia."

"Set Chronolocation for Lynchburg, Virginia. Spring of 1856. That gives us a few months to track our man and bring him home. Chrono jump in 3....2......"

A plasmatic burst marks the teams leap forward again on the stream.

# Chapter 8

The forests of Lynchburg, Virginia 1856

'Click, click, click.' The sound of a Colt 45's revolving cylinder as Marion mindlessly spent it while reviewing the plan he had set for his attack on the next plantation on his list. Thirty acres of land. Click. Various farm animals and cattle. Click, click. One multi room mansion. Click. One storage barn. Click. Occupants of the residence. Click. One husband. Click. One wife. Click. One child, a daughter. Click. Ten armed guards are placed strategically around the property. One overseer. Click, click, click. Thirty or so slaves. Click. Best method of approach is from the western front, utilizing the forest for cover upon approach to the property. Silently execute the overseer and any other combatants. Click. Prep explosives in the fields for escape diversion. Click. Enter the home via the window on the west wall. Execute interior guards and any other combatants. Disable door locks and jams to prevent escape. Click. Eliminate all targets. Click. Set fire to flammable materials inside the residence. Push to the slave quarters and quick review of occupants. As he combed over the details his mind's eye began to drift to better times.

The memory of a beautiful face and almond brown skin of a woman unfurls and commands his full attention. Her clothes were ragged and torn but she retained her regal aura regardless of the condition of her living. She was curvaceous with ample breasts that defied gravity's continuous tug on the human body and hips that beckoned any man's most sexually driven desires to the point it made men physically drool at the sight of her and then there were her eyes. Those emerald jewels sparkled in her sockets. A pleasant compliment to her heavenly beauty and was just as captivating as they were warm and inviting. Her smile radiated brighter than the sun on the hottest day of the year. She was soft and yet hardened from years of intense working and physical labor, too much for a man let alone a woman to endure but she did gracefully. Even the scent of her hair was intoxicating.

Kauchee was her name and she was his wife. His second chance at love in a strange place, in a strange time. The portion of his heart that he assumed had died and withered away suddenly was in full bloom like a flower bud during the first days of spring. She possessed a soul as beautiful as she. So, nothing could have captured his heart more than when she announced she was with child. The opportunity of such a blessing that bypassed him in his original timeline. His daughter, a glorious mashup of he and Kauchee's features, but she was especially blessed with her mother's stunning green eyes and the slight imperfection that made hers unique.

Gray skies rolled into the theater in his mind as the images changed from his singular source of joy to a vision of grim and bleak times. Kauchee's bloodied and lifeless body hung by her wrist from the whipping post. Ruby red stained the emerald of her irises. The back of her blouse was peeled open and matted to her battered flesh by the blood that had long since dried. That sight brought Marion to his knees and he wept uncontrollably desperately, wishing it was he instead of her that was drug back to this place and subjugated to this means of punishment. She died as a result of a decision. A decision that he made on everyone's behalf to escape to freedom. A decision where his wife and daughter deserved better than being slaves. A decision that ultimately ended her life as well as his. That torrent of pain welled up inside of him crashing into his most vulnerable parts and turning him cold and hard as ice. Coating his heart in its frigid grasp and then rage. Rage like he'd never felt before. A rage not even felt when he was informed that his wife of the present time was murdered during that home invasion on that fateful day. This blinding rage instantly pushed him to his mental limits. A hell storm sparked by traumatic experiences, a murderous all-consuming inferno that burned away everything good in a man until there was nothing left but ash and ruins. And from this, the lore was birthed.

Marion snapped out of his trance recognizing that his jaws were clenched together so tightly that his teeth were grinding. He finished checking his weapons and gear. The plan was to head out at zero dark thirty. Warriors possess the ability to toggle feelings and emotions on and off like a light switch, at a whim. It's the best way to deal with the killings. Shut that part of the brain down, compartmentalize it and process those feelings at a later date. But since the day he lost his second wife and child the internal knob in him had been permanently switched off. There was that brief period where he let his guard down and the end result is something he'll regret until he breathes his last breath.

Marion snapped the revolver cylinder back in its place and slid the cold blue steel into its worn leather holster. It was almost time to move out. The residents of the plantation lived in a sleepy sector of the town and had nestled into bed hours ago. They were sound asleep, none the wiser that death had pulled their ticket and was circling like a starved predator. The guards stood on post vigilantly, but they wouldn't have stand a chance even if they slacked on the job because they were staring hell in the face. The cattle stirred in their holding pens aware that something was headed that way due to some supernatural sixth sense. The birds in the trees still moved about as if it were not a quarter until 1 am. Wings flapping, and displaced chirping drew curious gazes from the guards. A cold chill blew in and the unpleasant odor of death with it. The overseer felt a lump forming in the pit of his stomach as he peered out his window into the night sky blanketed with overcast clouds that never fully transferred into rain. Just the pending gloom that seemed to settle over the property now. The feeling caused the overseer to grip his rifle tighter with both hands as the night progressed.

An almost inhumane shrill of pain from somewhere beyond his bedroom windows thrusted the plantation owner out of his slumber. His wife clung to him in fear and he did his best to calm her nerves as he stilled his own, while he rambled through the drawer of the nightstand by his bed searching for the pistol he kept stowed away there. He sprang to his feet. Another shriek, closer than the last one, made his heart almost spring from his chest. He forced a dry swallow down his throat as he swung open the bedroom door and crept out. A salvo of gunshots illuminated the hall and the foyer downstairs as bullets peppered the drywall, casting down a cloud of white dust like a creeping fog. The madam sat up clenched with fear, the blankets coiled up around her neck, the only thing she could think to do as her husband stumbled back into their bedchamber clutching his chest. Dots of crimson expanding across his nightgown. A wisp of smoke wafted up from the muzzle of his pistol signaling that he had traded gunfire with someone or something until it had run dry.

He struggled with his declining condition, reduced to dragging himself by his forearms along the wall back to the nightstand where more rounds were stored. A thunderous crack split the air as maroon mist stained the edges of the silk lined bedspread. The woman watched as her husband collapsed in a heap on the floor and a gaping hole was drilled through his skull. Behind him standing in the doorway with his pistol still drawn aimed in her direction was the Phantasm. Not a figment of her imagination but an actual man. He was no longer concerned with the mister of the house and now trained his focus on the mistress. Tears streamed down her ghostly pale cheeks making her eyes glassy.

" Please, No ..."

The reflections in her eyes exposed a view of a flurry of muzzle flashes. Plumes of red soiled goose feathers wafted from the mound of stuffed pillows decorating her bed. Gently floating and finally settling on her lifeless corpse.

In the blazing orange glow of the magnificent house fire, traces of the last slaves of the former plantation owners vanishing into the woods.

# Chapter 9

The servants of the Levy plantation adhere to a strict regimen which is carried out daily. First order of business each morning, Mr. Levy requires a fresh steaming pot of premium coffee. He's impossible to deal with prior to his first two cups and the entire household is aware of that even down to his children, who purposely steer clear of their father until he's had his morning brew.

The robust aroma of the dark brewed liquid jolted his senses to life as the first sips rushed over his palate, coating his taste buds in its exotic elixir. Mr. Levy was enjoying the caffeine rush when he observed what appeared to be smoke in the distance over the treetops. At first his mind couldn't comprehend what he was actually seeing but the reality of it smacked him like a bull stampede. The Culpeppers plantation was less than 5 miles up the road from his and the ominous column of smoke rising above the treetops confirmed his worst fears. The plantation was burning, presumably through the night.

A guard of his own rushed into the kitchen ready to deliver a message that Mr. Levy was already privy to. "Sir, you seeing this! I think it's the Culpeppers place. What do....?"

"Get guns, horses and men! Now!" shouted Mr. Levy, over the guard's yammerings as he moved to the front door.

Mrs. Levy, curious about what was causing the commotion so early in the morning she stepped out of the front door onto the porch with intentions to address it. She immediately covered her mouth with her hand, a gasp escaping through the gaps in her fingers, as she digested the sight. She found her husband, who stepped over to her and took her hand in his to comfort the tidal wave of fear rising up that would soon crash the shores of her mind, drowning out hope for the future. Or perhaps it was he who needed reassurance.

Minutes later the guard came trotting around the corner of the house guiding three horses by their reins in one hand and multiple long rifles tucked under his other arm. The horse reared up neighing as the rider pulled back hard on the straps. Two men scurried off the porch hurriedly reaching the rider to take hold of a rifle and horse. One held Mr. Levy's horse steady while he mounted it and once settled in the saddle he was handed his personal rifle.

The quartet sped off towards the smoke column ill-prepared for what they would encounter. The ride felt quicker than usual, the sounds of those horse's hooves were drowned out by the sounds of the men's beating hearts. Rounding a bend in the road, from a distance John could see a gathering of citizens just outside of the wooden fence, outlining the edge of the Culpeppers property. The sheriff and his men handled the growing crowd while the town's fire department extinguished the blaze. John found the Sheriff overwhelmed with statements from witnesses as well as coordinating the undertakers who dealt with collection of the deceased.

"Sheriff!"

"John Levy. Good morning. I don't think you'll be needing that, John, the threat has passed. We got a real hell of a mess on our hands, John." shaking his head sadly.

"Any survivors? Arlo? Mary? Betty?"

The Sheriff was silent, the look on his face was somber; it said all that needed to be said. As the two men conversed, the crowds doubled in size, the anticipation mounting as the undertaker and his morgue staff carted out the first recovered corpse. The body rested on a two-man wooden hand cart lined with black rubber sheets above and below the body, meant to contain fluid spills and it also helped in sealing in extreme odors that a dead body produces. The smell of charred flesh is a scent that will never leave you. It imprints its putrid memory on your brain like a red-hot branding iron.

As the death workers passed by, their rhythmic bouncing in tow caused one of the corpses' partially charred hands to slope down from the cart. The hand was small and pale. A child's hand. The mothers in the crowd gasped, clutched their chest and some began to weep. A larger body was removed next. From the white fabric hanging over the edges of the cart it was clear that this was Mary. John followed the men carting her body away until she was placed in the back of the morgue's transport wagon. The whole while thoughts raced through his mind, what if this were his wife and kids that lay in those carts? His home, his business gone in minutes. His legacy, up in smoke. His name to be tacked on with the list of victims in this maniac's self-empowered murderous rampage.

John was lost in his thoughts when the Sheriff tapped him on the shoulder. The morticians were removing the final corpse from the home, larger than the rest. John stepped in their path and raised a hand stopping them. The workers looked to the Sheriff who subtly nodded. John grabbed the edge of the top covering and peeled back the rubber layer. The scent assaulted his nostrils before the sight of the corpse filled his vision. A large craterous hole all but collapsed the body's forehead. The eyes were damaged and sunk in due to exposure to the heat. The hair on its head was singed to the scalp. Most of the flesh on the face was burned away, the edges of flesh crisped and blackened but enough remained to identify that it was Arlo Culpepper.

"Friend, you and your family did not deserve this. May God rest your soul and that of your families. Until we meet again."

Anger, sorrow, regret and revenge. The melting pot of emotions bubbled up inside. The Sheriff rested a hand on John's shoulder as a means of comfort but Mr. Levy quickly shrugged him off.

"Sheriff. Now, I don't want to impede you and your men's work but this nuisance must be stopped! Less than five miles, Sheriff. My plantation is less than five miles from here. Five miles! Who's next to fill those carts? Me? My family? I will not have it! I'll die by my own rules before I allow this.... this demon to exact death on us!  If you can't devise a means to rid this town of that pest...."

"John, we don't even know who the culprit is …"

"You know got damn well who the culprit is! The house is burned to the ground. The family's slain. Did you get a statement from the slaves?"

"No, John, there aren't any slaves here to question. They were gone before we arrived this morning. Clive has his dogs and hunters out now tracking their scents."

"You know what this is, Sheriff."

"Now c'mon now, John, I don't believe in that got damn black fairytale bullshit."

"How else do you explain this, Sheriff? John asked exasperatedly. "The attack was in the dead of night. The house, the family, the slaves are free. It's him. It's the Black Phantasm!"

"Even if it is, how the hell am I supposed to track a gotdamn ghost, John??"

"You're not equipped too, Sheriff. But I know someone who can and will, gladly."

~ ~ ~ ~

The mood in downtown Lynchburg was
ominous. The untimely passing of the Culpeppers
was a shock to the system. The Culpeppers were
considered friends to some, family to others but
without doubt a part of the community. Hearts were
definitely laden as Mr. Levy's horse slowly trotted
through the square. He stopped and dismounted in
front of the town's brothel.

As he tied his horse to the post and fed him
a few cubes of sugar, the gaggle of prostitutes
surrounding the door and walkway cat called him.
Offering their well-used orifices and remarkably
perky bodies up for a nominal fee. The promise of
promiscuity the likes a man has never known. The
brazen ones upped the ante with the dangling bait
of unsheathed bouncing breasts, free up skirt views
of bare bottoms and simulations of fellatio utilizing
theirs or their coworkers' fingers. These women
knew the men in town, especially the ones with
money and Mr. Levy was at the top of their 'To Do'
list. Mr. Levy declined all advances instead
inquiring with the Madam of the house the
whereabouts of a temporary resident. It only took
the description of the resident for the Madam to
immediately identify him. She rolled her eyes in

disgust and thumbed them in the direction of the second floor window overlooking the courtyard.

The madam seductively followed John to the base of the stairway, slithering with all the grace of a king cobra, as he ascended to the second level. She bit down on the tip of one of her long fingernails, tracking him with her eyes until he had turned the corner. She lovingly reminded him that she would be waiting downstairs with two sets of moist lips if he had a change of heart.

The door to Dunner's room was cracked and when John knocked on the door it partially opened with an annoying creak.

"C'mon in."

Dunner was cleaning himself up in the mirror. Splashing handfuls of water over his face and neck. He reached for a towel to wipe his brow. A young woman sat crouched in the corner as far from him as she could possibly be in the small room. Her makeup was running, making it appear as though the woman were crying black tears. The painted ruby red of her lips was smudged into streaks that reached way past the corners of her mouth. Ugly brown bruises shown along her neckline and down onto her chest and probably below that. She pulled up her panties and smoothed out her dress with her hands when John entered the room. As soon as he stepped in she grabbed the few dollars crumpled up on the floor at her feet and scurried out past him like a trapped mouse who'd suddenly been given an exit.

"Pardon my intrusion, Mr. Dunner, but I've come with pressing matters. It would appear our little problem has manifested itself last night. The Culpeppers, a family near and dear to mines, were brutally executed last night in the same fashion that fits the motive of the Black Phantasm."

Dunner stared at John through the mirror for a second before he turned to face the man. He wanted to make sure the look in John's eyes were sincere and they were.

"Got damnit! I knew it, I just knew it!"

He threw the towel down then rushed to his bed side to strap on his pistol and hurried to fit his boots on.

"Take me to the scene of the crime. I gotta see it for myself!"

By the time they arrived at the Culpeppers the crowd had dispersed and only law enforcement remained. Dunner took in the sight of carnage, silently observing. His gaze moved from the house towards the smoldering fields and back to the home's skeletal remains.

"This was him! This is that bastard's calling card. He's not done either. He's just beginning but this is his last gotdamn one. As God is my witness I'll see to that!"

"Do you have a plan?"

"Yes, I do. It's gonna take the entire community's assistance. Now I'm not gonna lie, Mr. Levy, but your hands are gonna get bloody. I need for you to understand this. Spread the word there's going to be a town hall meeting at noon tomorrow. Also, there's one more thing. I'm going to need the slave owners to come together and donate a few of their blacks for a demonstration."

# Chapter 10

As Mr. Levy was drumming up a solution for the town's problem, Mrs. Levy was attempting to gather her nerves and reinstate her home's tranquility. She decided she would do her part and prepare a sumptuous dinner with all the trimmings. No need to disrupt the normal routine. That would only aid in instilling fear in her family and she was stronger than that. She would prove that to everyone but more importantly to herself. She commanded the servants to bring out the fine China dishes and golden silverware. There were a few ingredients she was missing in the preparation of her family dinner that she absolutely required but she didn't have the time to make the store run herself. It would take hours that she didn't have to waste. Her nearest neighbors were a little over 3 miles away. This would be her best option at acquiring those ingredients.

At that moment Kyra entered the kitchen from outside carrying a pot full of freshly picked potatoes that were part of this evening's dinner. Mrs. Levy knew of her husband's infidelities with this young slave wench but she also knew her place in the hierarchy and mentioning his indiscretions would only make her look weak and insecure. The wife of a wealthy slave owner, jealous of an insignificant slave girl, the thought was ridiculous. However, the sentiment still remained. There was a killer on the loose and her venturing out would put her in danger, but this black girl's life mattered less than that of her family pets.

"Aye gal, I'm missing some key ingredients needed to complete my dinner. There's not enough time to make a store run with this killer on the loose. You go and get a bag and venture over to the Wallace's estate and ask Mary if she has the things on this list," thrusting a small piece of paper in the young girl's rough hand.

"The Wallace's ma'am? They don't take kindly to blacks roaming on their...."

"Hush up, girl! Now I know you aren't attempting to talk back to me? My husband would not be pleased to hear a slave disrespecting his wife."

"No ma'am, I wasn't...."

"Good! Take this list and this note as well. Just in case you have a run in with slave patrols. This will inform them you ain't no runaway. Now hurry up gal and go, you're holding up my dinner plans. Hurry back."

Kyra did not wish to leave the plantation alone; it wasn't safe for blacks at this time with the whites of the town being stirred up into a frenzy. The Wallaces were notorious for killing their own slaves and harming blacks in general for little to no reasons at all. And she highly doubted that her being property of the Levy's would be enough to stave physical abuse from those people. She'd have to be on her best behavior but she knew she faced a greater threat disobeying Mrs. Levy's commands. Stuck between a rock and a hard place, Kyra reluctantly grabbed a satchel. Being mindful enough to keep her facial expressions in check and stuffed the ingredient list as well as Mrs. Levy's written note in the front pocket of her dress and set off on her task. She said a quick silent prayer for safe travels as her bare feet graced the red dirt road.

It truly was a beautiful day despite the perceived tragedy that had taken place. The sun was high in the sky and the breeze was warm and inviting. Birds chirped happily above her. The sweet smell of summer flowers mingled together encircling her, constructing a moment of peaceful bliss that her young, tormented life needed more than she could have ever known. The quiet walk gave her time to reflect on things. The loss of her parents at an incredibly young age. Being a slave and sex object to such a vile man and the fact that she sees no foreseeable way of escaping this, nothing short of death. But then there's moments like this where everything seems to be in tune and in perfect harmony.

Her mind clashed with her love for God and the puzzling concept that she was loved by God but yet a slave. As her young mind wandered, her attention was captured by a bright blue feathered bird singing loudly on a tree branch off to the side. Below where the bird sat perched was a blossoming of honeysuckle plants exemplary and unblemished. The sweet sticky juice stored at the base of the flowers pistol released a mouthwatering aroma that was undeniably inviting. Kyra bundled the bright white flowers in her hand and drank in their intoxicating scent. She carefully picked and plucked a handful of them, being mindful not to remove more than what she deemed necessary. She plucked the little yellow stems from the center of the bottom bell of the flower and sucked out the nectar. Each flower only contained a few drops but each flower was a blessing to her taste buds.

Eventually she arrived at the Wallaces and was met with the business end of a double barrel shotgun courtesy of Mr. Wallace as he stepped out onto his front porch. Naturally the residents of Lynchburg were on edge but this was beyond ridiculous. Kyra, with shaky hands, protested that she brought no harm and she'd been sent on a task from Mrs. Levy at the Levy's plantation to gather things for a grandiose dinner planned for this evening. It wasn't until Mrs. Wallace and the headhouse servant stepped outside that Mr. Wallace relented and lowered the shotgun. Kyra handed the two notes to Mr. Wallace because she didn't have the ability to read and therefore had no idea which piece of paper was on the list.

Once Mr. Wallace realized Kyra's intentions were true; he commanded his servants to gather the things on the list. Kyra awaited nervously on the porch as her satchel was filled with the necessary items. Minutes later the house servant returned with her bag and handed it off to her instructing the young girl to get back home and make it quick.

"Hurry child and get on back to where you came from and don't be messing around. These white folks on edge and looking for blood. That damn Mrs. Levy is a scoundrel for sending a young gal out on her own after a morning like we had."

Kyra nodded, said yes ma'am and thanked the elder before turning, almost running off the plantation back to the road. Once she was out of sight of the Wallace home, she breathed a sigh of relief. The sun was lower in the sky now at this time but according to her calculations she would make it back to the plantation long before the sun set. At the halfway point she spotted another fruit bearing bush, this one was glistening fresh black berries. Again, her cravings took command of her and she found herself plucking the ripe plump fruits from the bush, savoring the sweet and tangy berries as they burst in her mouth. She made the mental note of creating an excuse to make more solo runs up this road so she could indulge in these natural born treats. Unbeknownst to her, she was about to cross paths with a roving group of slave patrollers and regularly armed angry white men.

She heard the horses before she spotted the men but by the time that happened it was too late. She recognized the silver stars pinned to the shirts of a few of them instantly recognizing who they were. Her hands moved to the front pocket of her dress where her lifeline, the handwritten note from Mrs. Levy was stored. Her heart sank to the bottom of her stomach when she discovered that the pocket was empty. She had both notes and she knew she had both notes when she left earlier that day. Fear, like a flash freeze, instantly seized her as her mind retraced her steps. Then it hit her. At the Wallaces she'd handed off both letters to Mr. Wallace and he never returned either of them. The slave patroller leading the pack dismounted his horse and ambled her way periodically glancing over his shoulder back at the other men. Kyra trembled in his shadow as he drew closer. This man reeked of booze and sun-baked body odor as he circled her. The dull glimmer from his tin star was the focal point of her eyes.

"In Virginia it's illegal for slaves to roam free in the township of Lynchburg without proper paperwork. Do you have paperwork on your person?"

Kyra with trembling motions shook her head.

"I had a note but I... I must've misplaced it. I come from the Levy's plantation and I was sent on a food run for the my missus to the Wallace's up the road there. I'm on my way back to the Levy's now, sir, I'll be on my way."

She went to take a step past the man and he shifted his body into her path. The fear in her was steadily rising. She was so terrified that she trembled under his judgmental gaze. He raised rutty hand to her face grazing his filthy fingers over the soft skin of her jaw.

"Didn't know you monkeys made pretty babies but, you are quite the eye full ain't ya?"

Kyra said nothing and stood there as she fought back the tears formulating. His touch felt so wrong to her. She could feel in her heart that this man had ill intentions for her. She silently prayed for safe passage. The slave patroller's hand traced her cheek down the side of her neck and along the edge of her shoulder, noticing the tremble that became uncontrollable. His hand glided over her forearm to her wrist and their fingers touched briefly before he yanked the satchel out of her hand. A tiny yelp escaped her mouth but then she returned to silence.

"Seford, would you kindly check this satchel?"

A stocky man on horseback slid down off his saddle and took the bag, rambling through its contents.

"Food, bread, some vegetables, spices and herbs and a slab of bacon," inhaling deeply, "or salted pork belly."

He wiped his mouth with the back of his hand as he unraveled the seasoning meat and bit a large bite from the pork slab, obnoxiously smacking on the semi cooked meat greedily. That was an important part of Mrs. Levy's dinner. A twinge of anger flared up in the young girl but it was smothered by overwhelming fear.

"Well, you're not a liar and that's a good thing. But are you a thief? How do we know you didn't steal this food from the Wallaces, or the Levy's for that matter. Now, I can oversee this series of violations, if..."

He raised his hand to her cheek again, caressing her face and tilting her head back so he could take in the fullness of her beauty. His hand moved swiftly to her neck restricting her breathing and with his other hand he ripped at the collar of her dress. She screamed, ear piercing like a banshee's wailing and kicked at the slaver's knee. The organic hinge buckled as pain flared up causing the man to release his grip. In that split second Kyra made the decision to flee to the woods as fast as her feet would carry her away from those men.

"Get her!!"

The group charged into the woods behind her. She was shorter and more nimble than the rugged men which made her able to move over downed tree limbs and under tangled rope vines. One of the men drew his pistol and fired a shot that burrowed into the trunk of a tree inches from her head. Adrenaline coursed through her veins as she sprinted for dear life.

She gained distance on her pursuers which only angered them further as more of them drew firearms and began shooting at her. A burst of tree bark debris clouded her sight, disorienting her which caused a misjudgment in her steps. Her bare feet slipped on a slick wet surface and before she knew it she was tumbling over end down a steep slope.

The only thing she could hear besides the rush of blood in her ears, was the sounds her body made bouncing over the jagged terrain. Her pain receptors overloaded, and she lost consciousness. Her chasers skidded to a stop at the top of the ravine and with huffing breaths peered over the edge scanning left to right for a trace of her but due to the narrow valley and its uneven walls that made it impossible to see anything beyond a few feet below. They could hear the river's torrents and naturally assumed the girl fell and drowned. Or she's floating down stream into open country where a bear or a mountain lion would make short work of her. Confident that's what happened the men turned and headed back up the hill towards the roadway.

Sometime later that evening Kyra's body had washed up on the river's shores. She was still alive, unconscious and banged up a little with a small quantity of water in her lungs but alive. A figure wearing black fur wrapped footwear akin to moccasins stood over top of her sleeping body. This sleeping beauty was strangely familiar to him even though he couldn't pinpoint the reasons why. It was something about her face that seemed vaguely familiar. The figure noticed the bruises and scrapes decorating her little body. She had fallen from somewhere and landed in the river. No telling how long she floated but it was her luck that she beached up on the riverbank here. A set of strong hands reached down and very tenderly scooped her up into their arms and turned back into the woods.

# Chapter 11

Hours later Kyra's eyes fluttered open. She was in an unfamiliar place. She had a clear view of the sky above. A galactic gala of celestial bodies set with a pure black backdrop and rolling purple clouds. Her body registered heat from a nearby campfire and as her senses came back to focus, she could smell the scent of meat and vegetable stew brewing. Her stomach growled as a response to the delightful scents.

Her body tensed up when she noticed the man sitting on the other side of the fire staring at her. He was black and big. Instinctively she pushed away, backing into the wide base of a gnarled tree. She couldn't believe she'd ended up getting caught after all she had been through but then her mind settled on a singular thing. This man sitting across from her was a Black man. He was carving potatoes into thin medallion slices and dumping them into the stew. He wore a black handkerchief around his neck and a nubuck coat with a bandelier strapped over his chest with a pistol attached and another bandelier around his waist with another matching pistol, black nubuck pants and fur wrapped boots. A long gun lay resting up against the tree behind him. Kyra watched him for a while as he worked before, he spoke to her.

"You were out for a nice while. Few hours. Got a nice bump on your head but nothings broken or bleeding badly, so you're lucky. What are you doing out here alone, little girl, you have to know this isn't safe out here."

She remained quiet.

"What's your name? Are you hungry?"

She stayed quiet, eyes wide as fear held her. Her primal senses began to engage after a while; it was the smell of that meat roasting on the open flame. The scents of that vegetable stew mingling with the other delicious fragrances made her stomach feel as though it were a beast rattling its confinement. She also remembered she had been sent out on a task by Mrs. Levy and every passing hour spelled doom for her and her loved ones back at the plantation. She struggled to get to her feet but found it was easier said than done. The bump on her head had her dizzy and exhausted. The stranger protested that she relaxes and regains her strength before attempting to stand and leave. At this point it would only cause more damage along with the fact it was nighttime. Traversing through the woods at night provided another level of obstacles she was not ready to face. He gestured with his hands for her to sit. He returned to his cooking and before long it was as if the stranger could read her mind because he ladled a bowl of the stew and cut off a generous portion of the meat, plopping it into the stew. He took a cup and filled it with water and brought the items over to her, placing them down at her feet. Then he got up and walked back to his side of the camp and made his portions. Kyra wasted no time diving into the bowl of vittles. The flavors were a barrage of experiences clashing in her mouth. She was used to eating the scraps and discarded pieces of meat, the spoiled or withered vegetation and fruit given to her by her owners. The flavors of fresh had no comparison.

"Hey, HEY, whoa slow down. You're gonna choke. There's plenty to go around. If you're still hungry, there's plenty."

Embarrassed at her behavior she wiped her mouth with the sleeve of her dress and gulped down mouthfuls of the surprisingly cool spring water. "Pardon me, mister. Thank you. This meal is the most delicious food I have ever eaten. My momma would be ashamed of the way I behaved. My name is Kyra. What's your name, mister?"

"Marion."

She nodded and continued eating. He did the same. They ate till their bellies were full then just like that Marion turned over and soon was snoring, soundly asleep. Kyra guzzled the last of her water and shuffled closer to the campfire. Before long she was drifting off to dreamland herself.

Meanwhile back at the Levy's plantation, Mr. Levy had just returned home to find Mrs. Levy visually disturbed in the kitchen as she threw dirty pots and pans across the counter into the sink.

"What in the hell are you doing? Why are you tossing them pots and pans like a mad woman?

Mrs. Levy was so upset that tears formed as Mr. Levy caught her hand before she tossed another soiled pot.

"I wanted to prepare you a special meal to take your mind away from the horrible things going on in our town. I was missing some ingredients and

93

asked that damn little black bitch to travel to the Wallaces and retrieve what I needed. She ain't returned and now, my dinner's ruined."

Mr. Levy consoled her in his arms, calming her down.

"What gal you sent darling. You let me know and I promise I'll punish them for upsetting my darling wife, so."

"That little nigga wench Kyra!"

John's eyebrows raised up. He wasn't prepared to hear his sex slave was missing. All kinds of thoughts raced through his mind. Was she dead? Did she flee? The Black Phantasm was out there, did she run into him. Was she part of his movement? Would they be heading to their home next? These thoughts accumulated in his mind as his temper increased. He released his wife and stormed out the front door towards the slave quarters, bursting in the door as the slaves ate their meager meals. He scanned the crowd before storming out and into the next home. John repeated this over and over until he laid eyes on each of his slaves and Kyra wasn't present among any of the homes. This made his blood boil. Not just the fact that his wife had sent his prize slave out into the world alone but that Kyra's ungrateful ass hasn't returned and that she might actually be attempting to flee to Freedom town.

His mind raced with ideas and solutions when the voice of Dunner echoed in his mind. 'I'm going to need the slave owners to donate a few slaves.' John rushed back to the main slave quarters searching for a particular person. Kyra's adoptive mother. He spotted her sitting at one of the tables and yanked her up by her arm.

"Where is she??"

"Where's who massa?? Please massa I beg you for mercy!"

"Where is Kyra! She's a runner! She headed to freedom town?

"I don't know, I don't know massa please! Mercy massa "

The woman shook her head vigorously. Mr. Levy is sporadic when he's upset and unfortunately, they've all witnessed his rage. The other slaves gasped in fear, pleading with their master. They feared the woman had displeased Master Levy although they couldn't discern why. The overseer came in behind John and snatched up two more slaves then stormed out threateningly gesturing with a long rifle for the slaves to remain seated as they left.

The next morning Kyra awoke to a series of stiff taps on her shoulder. She squinted in the blinding light of the day as she recognized where she was. Marion was fully dressed and appeared ready to escort her home. She pushed herself up on her butt and sat for a second gathering her thoughts. Marion retrieved another cup of water and offered it to her but paused when their eyes met. He studied hers for abnormally long before releasing the cup. He continued staring as if he recognized her only breaking away from his gaze when he heard branches snap in the distance. It was a deer or something that didn't immediately demand his attention.

"How's your head feeling?"

Kyra touched the tender spot on her scalp wincing at the sensation. It was still tender to the touch but not as bad as it was the day before. She nodded slowly and stood to her feet. The whole world shifted left to right a few times but finally settled back on center but a swift shaking cleared the cobwebs. Marion extended a hand that seemed to stabilize her world in an instant. The plantation was several miles away and they trekked in relative silence over the mountainous terrain intentionally avoiding the roadway because of Kyra's previous encounter. The mountains were peaceful. For a long while there was nothing but the sounds the leaves and branches made crunching under their feet. Finally, it was Marion that broke the silence.

"You have unique eyes for a black girl. Green eyes but what's most peculiar is that bit of gray in the corner."

"I get my eyes from my momma .... God rest her soul, that's what my new momma tell me. She said my momma was beautiful and had the same eyes like jade jewels cut and placed right in our heads."

"Yea very unique. I have seen eyes like this before but it was a long time ago. Is your father around?"

Her eyes dropped to the ground as sorrow swelled in them causing an almost unstoppable flow of tears. She was able to corral her feelings long enough to push those emotions back in, back down. She drew a few breaths then answered.

"My father is dead. So is my momma. Killed when I was young. I was too young to remember. My new mama, Mama B took responsibility of me when I was a baby and I been hers ever since. Lawd I pray for her. I been gone all night and I never returned with Mrs. Levy's goods. Got a nasty feeling in the pit of my stomach, mister."

Marion didn't respond; he just nodded as they kept pushing through the forest. He was distracted with his own thoughts. This young girl with those eyes. Those distinct eyes. Could it be? Is it even possible? He lost his wife and his baby girl that horrible night. Right? This could be her, after all these years. She looks about the right age. The father inside of him wanted to thrust open his arms and embrace his long-lost daughter but he had to be rational. He has to confirm this first or it will freak this kid out. She's been through so much at such a young age. And he has been through so much too in his life even before the accidental time jump. But even just this period right now to find love and lose love for a second time is something no person should experience once let alone twice. It will drive you to madness. This whole murderous rampage of his is the direct result of that. He's been following the path of the underground headed north in search of what he had no idea still existed. And becoming the vengeance that these people seek but never could obtain. Dr Stansfield warned him to be gentle with his interactions in the time stream because they could alter the future. All positive intentions died that night his wife and daughter were taken from him.

But now if this is his long-lost daughter, this changes things. His mission was one of selfish purpose to begin with. If this is his daughter, then the killings can end. After this last stop. Kyra is concerned about the wellbeing of her foster parent as well as the other slaves on the plantation. This is the last one Marion thought to himself.

The thoughts and potential outcomes of decisions he has made pace through his mind. It was a long while before he noticed Kyra was looking at him.

"You ok, mister? You been quiet like you thinking bout something real hard."

"Yea. Yes, I'm fine…. Kyra, I need to say something…." But his words were cut short when they heard the sounds of many people talking near the roadway. Marion squatted and pulled Kyra down with him placing a finger over his lips. He craned his neck to angle his ear for better reception. The crowd of men and women were discussing the meeting to take place at town square at noon. Marion looked up at the sky for the sun's positioning. It was almost in the center of the sky which meant whatever this meeting was about, would be starting soon.

One person mentioned they knew the meeting was about the plague known as the Black Phantom and that someone in town had a solution to rid them of the problem. Marion wanted to keep his daughter safe, but this town hall meeting was about him. A solution to rid the town of him? He had to spy on it.

"Listen, it's nearly noon. I know I said I would escort you home and I will but first I have to see what this town hall meeting is about for your safety and the safety of every other black person in this town."

"But why, mister? Them white folks talking don't concern us. They gone do what they gone do with us regardless. That Black Phantom is a God sent if you ask me."

"Kyra, is there a vantage point where I can see what's going on in the town and still remain undercover?"

"Well yes, there is a bluff on the edge of town overlooking the river that runs alongside the town. You can see the center of town from that point."

"Take me there."

The bluff was shrouded with tall grass and low hanging tree limbs making for a perfect cover. It sat about 60 feet at its highest point overlooking the river as Kyra said. By the time Marion had scaled the bluff he could see a stage was set up in the center of town and people were already gathering as more people were arriving. Marion used the makeshift scope he attached to his rifle and scanned the crowd. The sheriff and deputies were in attendance along with the mayor and his cabinet.

Lynchburg, Town Center

Dunner stood at the edge of the platform as the crowd grew in size. The people became chatty as they developed their own reasoning behind the town hall meeting. Mr. Levy materialized in the crowd. He had two of his guards and three slaves with him. The slaves were troubled not knowing why they were chosen to accompany Mr. Levy, but they knew that nothing good would come from it as their hearts froze, like petrified wood, when they spotted the stage. The mayor made his way to Mr. Levy when he saw him and Dunner speaking and after shaking hands speaking briefly Dunner took the stage. His hard bottom boots clacked as he climbed the stairs and crossed to center stage. He turned and nodded at Mr. Levy who then instructed his guards, who shoved the three slaves of his towards the steps.  They shuffled up them and towards Dunner with their heads hung low.

"Citizens and town folk of Lynchburg. I am Morgan Dunner. I know the potential problem you all face with this Black Phantasm. My sincerest condolences to the Wallaces and the impact of that family's horrific murders has on all of you standing here today. I too have been affected by the evil deeds of that Black demon almost 2 decades ago. I was a wealthy businessman myself. Owning a burgeoning plantation, I specialized in production and processing of cotton. I had a wife and children of my own. I know the stinging pain of losing it all and trust me I have the scars inside and outside to prove it, but I have a solution. I've been tracking this sum bitch for years, always one step behind him. Now, he's a man, just a man and nothing more. But this man possesses talents that make him a bit more difficult to dispose of but in the end he's just a man like me. Men are slaves to their emotions. Anger, fear, and sadness being the most powerful of the lot. I've learned over the years that if you can control a man's emotions then you can control him like a wagon rider controls his horses with the reins. And I find that fear and anger, when used properly, are excellent means of motivation. When I was a child my father would have me help him hunt down the rodents that would plague our farm lands and I learned a very valuable lesson from killing all of those field mice, moles, foxes and what not. The best way to kill vermin is first you have to smoke them out of their hiding places."

With that Dunner pivoted on his heels and drew his pistol aiming at the first slave's head. A singular bead of sweat fell from the brow of that unsuspecting poor soul and without a second thought Dunner squeezed the trigger. The crack of the round echoed far beyond the city's walls up and over the bluff. The second round rocked the skull of the next slave in succession before the first one's body had hit the floor. As Dunner lined his pistol up with the forehead of the third slave, the older woman, for the final shot her eyes were wide and filled with terror as she was suddenly faced with her immediate and untimely demise. A high pitched scream from far away streaked across the square peeling away everyone's attention including Dunner's towards the direction of the scream. The bullet ignited but barely grazed the outside of the elderly woman's head, spraying a thin line of blood through the air. Dunner turned to see the woman roll over, holding the side of her head and staving off the flood of crimson erupting from her scalp.

He looked back at the bluff where the scream originated and smirked with evil glee as he thumbed the hammer back on his revolver and took aim on the defenseless woman. He leveled the gun at her head, his finger slipped into the trigger guard and caressed the cold steel. Before he could squeeze, a shot rang out and hot searing pain shot down his right arm. He'd been shot. The staccato of gunfire from overhead caused the crowd to scatter in a panic as Dunner cupped the outside of his arm. The white-hot pain sprinted down his arm, where the heat emanated from a bullet that passed though the fleshy portion of the shoulder.

On the bluff, Marion had been observing the whole scenario. They were positioned too far from the crowd to pick up any clear audio but he's engaged in enough conflicts to know the body language of a killer or killer intent. Kyra lay beside him watching as well.

"Mister, is that thing on top of your rifle, the looking glass, that makes things far away look like they right up on you? If so, can I take a peek through 'em?"

Marion turned his head to her. Her jade colored eyes seemed to radiate more vibrantly in the daytime reminding him again of his lost lover. He reached in a small satchel and pulled out a second telescope which he extended then handed it off to her. She propped herself up on her elbows and adjusted the eye piece as she looked over the crowd. Marion trained his focus on the men talking at the bottom of the stairs. He noticed in the sea of white people there, three blacks stood.

"That's my master! That's Mr. Levy down there standing by the stage! I can tell that evil face from a mile away." Kyra said with trepidation.

"Mr. Levy? The man that's claiming ownership over you?"
Kyra nodded and continued watching.

"And who are those black people with him?"

She shifted her focus to the three dark figures huddled behind the stage almost out of view of the crowd.

"I can't tell but they look out of place like flies in a bowl of milk."

Marion watched the Sheriff walk over to the men conversing and said something briefly before the man in all black took to the stage. As soon as the man turned towards the crowd Marion got the feeling that the man in black looked familiar to him but his features were seriously distorted due to scarring on his face. Whatever he said had the crowd captivated as he paced back and forth waving his hands about. Kyra watched in silence until the black trio marched on stage, that's when her heart almost leapt from her chest.

"What?! That's...that's my momma!" clutching the small telescope tightly.

Krya tried to scramble to her feet before the thoughts registered in her mind. It was Marion's swift and stern hand that caught her and brought her back down. He pressed her into the grass flattening her chest and gesturing to her to stay put and to calm down as he returned his focus back to the stage. Just then the first shot took him by surprise.

The second made the muscles of his body tense up with anger at the blatant cold murders. Krya screamed so loud that bells rang in Marion's ear. The scream echoed down below as the shooter's attention temporarily peeled away from his victim and towards the bluff. The stranger in black had missed his point blank shot due to the sudden high pitched noise, He turned and cocked the weapon reading it for a second shot. At that moment Marion's subconscious mind connected the face with a name.

"Dunner!"

He grinded his teeth and mumbled angrily under his breath as his finger slid from the frame of the rifle to hovering over the rigger.

"No! That's my momma! The only person I have left in this world! Do something, PLEASE!" Kyra pleaded brokenly.

Those words coming from Kyra burrowed into his heart but they soon hit the solid callus of hate that had grown over the organ over the past years. The origin of this calcification stood a little over a hundred yards away. A lifetime of regret and remorse flooded the portion of his brain related to logical thinking. Marion depressed the trigger and the large bore weapon bucked, hurling a .64 caliber round down range smacking into the shooter's shooting arm with tremendous force, knocking him to one knee.

The pistol skid across the stage and out of reach. Dunner tried to go for the gun when Marion adjusted his aim and fired a second shot puncturing the wooded stage just shy of Dunner causing him to pivot and find cover. Marion lost his target in the slew of stampeding citizens. He saw Mr. Levy reaching down and yanking up the wounded slave woman then vanished in the crowd as well.

"We gotta move. NOW!" Marion shouted but Kyra was in shock.
"Kyra! NOW!"

She still didn't budge. He wrapped his arm around her waist and lifted her petite frame to her feet. Taking her hand in his he sped down the bluff in leaps and bounds. He knew oh too well what came next. In the field once your position is exposed you evacuate ASAP, as the enemy usually will converge on your last known position. A combat scenario he's witnessed repeatedly through his military career although this was the first time he would be exfil with a noncombatant who also happens to be his only living relative in this time period. This is purely an escape and evade maneuver.

The Sheriff, from behind cover, commanded his men to rally at the bluff. "Flank the shooter and kill whoever took that shot."

Once the law men felt the coast was clear they separated and ran towards the bluff, keeping close to the buildings and objects using them for cover.

Marion usually moved slowly and methodically when passing through sensitive terrain like moist jungle grounds, fragile forest floors, snowy or muddy settings. A branch broken or hanging in an unnatural manner including a fresh unusual depression in the soft earth, or snow; any list of things could provide a skilled tracker with precious intel about the target. However, now wasn't the time for proper procedures.

# Chapter 12

A couple hours later a group of sweaty men, a combination of law men and armed citizens stomp through town square. The still nervous wrecks of townspeople parted the crowd to make way for the men as they headed to the doctor's office filing into the open space of the establishment where Dunner's wounds were being tended to.

The Doctor had examined the entry and exit wounds determining that it was a clean pass through. There was minimal bleeding for a gunshot with no ruptured vessels, arteries or broken bones. Dunner held a bottle of whiskey in his hand going back and forth between guzzling huge swigs to numb the pain and oscillating the brown liquor in the clear bottle as the doctor prepared a needle and thread.

"Mr. Dunner. Are you ready?"

Gesturing to the needle and thread, Dunner took another hard hit of the whiskey before dumping the remainder of the contents on his open wound. He bit down on a strip of thick rawhide as the distilled spirits sizzled with an intense heat sterilizing the damaged flesh. The doctor's pin needle point passed through; over and under, over and under, again and again cinching the wound shut then snipping the loose end of the thread. The doctor repeated the procedure on the other side of Dunner's shoulder and in minutes the operation was complete. A few dabs of sterile water on a damp cloth for the aftercare along with a fresh wrapping of bandages.

"Keep the wound and the surrounding area clean. Change the bandages frequently as possible and try to go easy on the arm, Mr. Dunner."

The nurse finished up as the doctor excused himself. The Deputy stepped forward as Dunner painstakingly slid his coat back on.

"So, lawman, you find anything of value out there?"

"Went up to the bluff. Found some evidence that someone had been prone watching for a good while. Tracks leading down the bluff into the forest, two sets of prints were discovered. One was indistinct, not a boot more like a moccasin but judging by the size and width of the prints they were men's and the other, barefoot, small, either a child or a small woman. We followed their tracks to the creek where we lost the trail. I have my best trackers roaming up and down the creek as we speak."

"They'll need more than guns and rifles if your men find him, but I got that covered. He's good but I'm better, thinking outside of the box. This time he's gonna come right to me. That nigger woman that I grazed, she's some kind of important for one reason or another. Maybe a relative or maybe he was just tired of seeing his kind be slaughtered like cattle. Either way the board is set. And he's got a tag-along now, added weight gonna slow him down. He's gonna come and when he does I'll be ready and waiting."

As night fell, groups of torch wielding trackers and armed white men scoured the forest in the search for any sign of the Black Phantasm. A trackers hound picked up a scent a while ago and they've been following the trail since. The crazed dogs darted back and forth through the underbrush as they hunted.

Marion and Kyra made it back to his camp deep in the woods near the mountains where he had stashed the bulk of his equipment and supplies. Years of war sharpens one's sixth sense and his was blaring like an emergency alarm. He knew a search party would be combing the valley probably at that very moment so time was of the essence. Marion was preoccupied gathering his gear and almost didn't notice Kyra who was becoming increasingly hysterical, tugging and pulling away from his grasp; her concern was not of her own safety but that of her mother's. Marion had to snatch her up and shake her until her anxiety subsided.

"Let me go! Let me go! He's gonna kill her! I can stop him. Or save her or...."

"YOU CAN'T! You can't save her.....but I can. I just need time to formulate a plan. They'll be waiting for me to show up. I no longer have the element of surprise on my side. Give me some time that's all I'm asking for."

Kyra calmed down but it was only a ruse. Once she felt Marion's grip relax her hands shot out faster than a rattlesnake's bite and ripped one of his pistols from its holster. Stepping back with trembling hands she pointed the hand cannon at his chest. Marion raised his hands towards the night sky. Tears streamed down Kyra's cheeks twinkling like tiny crystals illuminated by the pale dull glow of the crescent moon.

Marion softly spoke. "Listen, I know you're afraid of what's to come. I won't lie to you; it looks bleak but if you just trust me on this …"

"Trust you! Trust you! Mister, I don't even know you! You're supposed to be some big bad legend, a ghost, a phantasm. Yea, I know who you are! I'm not just some dumb little black girl! You've been killing and setting the wrongs right for my people but I haven't seen that yet! I'm still a slave and my momma almost died today. Those other two, God rest their souls but my momma is laying in her bed bleeding probably inches from death or worse. And you're running. Afraid!"

Marion lost it and the truth came spilling out.

"You want to know me? You want to know who I REALLY am! Ok, fine! I'm a murderer trained by Uncle Sam himself! I'm First Lieutenant Airman Marion Marks of the United States Air Force Pararescue from the 720th Special Tactics Division. I'm from the year 2040. I was part of a special team working on a secret project, time travel. I was equipped with a device that would allow me to move up and down the chronostream at will, at any point in the stream. My device had a catastrophic failure resulting in me being launched back in time

200 years to Santee, South Carolina. The device was destroyed in the time jump leaving me stranded in this time period.

The protective suit I was wearing somehow bonded with the cells of my body granting me a measure of invulnerability. Still, that didn't stop me from being captured by slavers. Even though I couldn't be killed by conventional methods it still hurt like hell. I was sold to a man where I would remain for the next two years. But in that time I met a woman.  She was beautiful with the most radiant green eyes. Green like ripe leaves in spring. Unique because they held a bit of grey in the corner of her right eye just like yours! She was my breath, my peace, my second chance at life. We found love with each other. Her name was Kauchee and she was your mother.

Soon she was with child. Our child. A girl. Crazy that I could find joy in a world like this, but I did. I found joy in her and my daughter. I decided it was time to leave, they deserved better than being slaves and I would be the one to deliver them to freedom town but we were sabotaged. The slave master caught wind of my plans and pursued us. In the chaos we were separated. She was taken back to the plantation while I was hunted down. They found me in the swamps and surrounded me. The slave master, Morgan Dunner, shot me in the head at point blank range. I should've died but that's when I found out I have this gift and curse. I awoke sometime later in that murky swamp. I made my way back to the plantation but when I arrived, what I saw, it broke me. My wife, My.... I was seething with hate at how they did her. What they did to her. I stalked up to the plantation killing every guard and any servants that dared to stop me. I killed the Master's wife, children, and him so I thought.

I felt the life drain from his body as I slid the blade deep into his chest. During the scuffle a candle was knocked over causing a fire to spread which consumed the house and eventually the fields. When I made it out to the slave quarters the slaves had all fled into the woods with my baby. I knew where they were headed but I never saw them again. I destroyed plantation after plantation banishing those evil men and women to hell as I searched for my daughter. I had given up all hope and fully invested myself, alone, in the mission of death and destruction. But when I saw you lying on that river's edge the other day I thought there was no way. But you're here. You're alive and I thank God, I thought I lost you ...."

Marion stepped forward, moisture glazing over his tired eyes and Kyra took a step back, raising the pistol again to his chest. This time she managed to cock back the hammer.

"What are you saying, Mister? You, you think you're my father??"

She busted out in hysterical laughter that took Marion by surprise.

"Mister, I believe you did take a knock on the head. My mother and father are dead. Mama Nancy B been my mother since that time, and she told me what happened to them."

"Momma Nancy B lied to you to protect you!"

"You don't know that. You just standing here right now talking to save your life. I'm going to the Levy's and you ain't stopping me. If you try, I swear for Lord I'll put a bullet in your head."

"What are you not getting, Kyra! I'm indestructible! I'm also your father! What do I have to do to prove this to you!"

Kyra said nothing, she just stood there in silence, the clattering from the pistol trembling in her hand blending in with the night's chorus. Marion came to a resolution and as quick as lightning before Kyra could react, he'd drawn the other pistol from the holster and placed the barrel on his temple. With no hesitation he locked eyes with her and pulled the trigger. The concussive blast was all but deafening in those woods. Kyra diverted her gaze when she saw what Marion was about to do, deciding she had seen enough death for one day. The blast sent a bolt of adrenaline coursing through her.

"Kyra, it's ok. Look, look at me."

Marion's voice was soothing. He didn't sound upset or like a man that had just blown off the top portion of his skull. She turned to face him and was amazed at the fact Marion was unharmed, not even a scratch.

"I told you. I'm indestructible. I'm not lying to you, Berry…."

"What…? What did you call me? How? How do you know that name? My name!?"

"Me and your mother gave it to you when you were born. It's because of the birthmark on your lower back. It's in the shape of a strawberry. Even has the tiny leaves that grow on them once they're ripe."

All Kyra could do was stand there in shock as she processed what this strange man was saying to her. Fifteen years she's lived alone in this world thinking her biological parents were dead and here comes along a man claiming to not only be her father but he hails from the future. It can't be. Can it? Her mind wrestled with the concept of what she'd just witnessed. He shot himself in the head to prove a point and the bullet didn't so much as phase him. Was he telling the truth about this as well?

Marion extended his hand to her; the open palm was a silent demand for the weapon still in her clutches. As his hand found hers, hers became soft and pliable. He gently peeled her fingers back and returned both pistols to their holsters and then pulled her into his strong embrace. Relief washed over both of them. This was an occurrence that had a one in a million chance.

Just then a branch snapped loudly in the darkness. Marion's eyes darted left to right then he noticed the crickets had stopped chirping, always a bad sign. Using his body as a shield he knelt down over his daughter placing him in between her and

119

the direction the disruption came from. Moments later a volley of rifle rounds ignited the pitch black surrounding them as a brigade of armed men opened fire on the two. Bullets pinged off of his impervious body as he cradled his daughter in his arms, the both of them shouting through the barrage.

"Don't move! Stay close, the bullets can't harm me!"

Hundreds of rounds were spent in the assault, so much in fact that gunsmoke and the scent of burnt sulfur hung low in the air mixing with the moisture, developing a fog like cloud that obscured the view of the battlefield. The shots ceased as the men surveyed the damage.

Each assaulter had been issued a few sticks of dynamite, a suggestion of Dunner's in the event the search parties encountered the Phantasm. A good call on his behalf. An assaulter drew his stick of dynamite and lit the fuse, waiting a few seconds before he tossed the explosive into the clearing.

Marion heard the sizzle of the fuse burning before he spotted it and he reacted the only way he knew how, turning his body into the path of the blast moments before the black powder went off. The blast enveloped them, hurling him and his daughter several yards into the brush. Marion

120

tucked in and rolled his body to absorb the brunt of the impact but it still caused the intertwined pair to bounce violently off the dirt. When they finally rolled to a stop Marion was disoriented and his vision was blurred. Him being invulnerable didn't impede the explosive properties of concussive force.

Internally he felt like he had stopped a speeding tractor trailer with his guts. The pain was excruciating but he had no time to recuperate as that familiar sizzling sound filled his ear canals again. He scooped his daughter in his arms and took a few steps before the blast sent him careening deeper into the forest. They were showered with bits of bark and dirt. Kyra coughed trying to catch her breath after the wind had been knocked out of her. A thin stream of blood trickled out of the corner of her mouth.

"Kyra, baby girl! You still with me?"

She nodded weakly. Marion guided his hand over her body checking for any bleeds, a technique he was taught in the military. His hands were dry which was a good sign but they weren't out of the woods yet. The darkness of the forest provided perfect cover to conceal their whereabouts from the assaulters but those men and their torches moved ever so close to him and his daughter. Marion had to get on the offensive and he had to NOW. A torch in pitch darkness is a bullet beacon. Marion laid his daughter down inside the concave portion of a naturally hollowed tree. Brushing the strands of curls from her sweet face and swiping away the remainder of blood besmirching her innocence. For her he was gentle, patient, loving. Years apart and he had to resolve to bury those emotions to stay alive long enough for this moment. For her, he would become the monster caged within. The monster the United States military created all those years ago. For her, he would burn this whole world down but tonight just these men will feel his wrath. They wanted a Black Phantasm, so be it.

# Chapter 13

The men cautiously stalked through the forest searching for Marion so they could finish the job unaware they were being stalked in turn. He truly became a shadow as he emerged from the dark void cast by the lofty trees. He had pulled the cloth over his face and become a true creature of the night. Soundless as a ghost, the first victim fell to his blade. He allowed the darkness to submerge him and he re-emerged behind another gunman seemingly teleporting from target to target.

The gunman wasn't swift enough to defend against the supernatural predator. Marion appeared behind the man and buried the blade of his knife into the soft portion of the shooter's neck where the Adam's apple met the clavicle. Muffled gurgles of a throat full of blood quickly dissolved into nothing as the man met his gruesome end. The sounds of that man's death rattles forced the other shooters to become on edge as light sources were snuffed out one by one.

Marion materialized, launching his dagger at another enemy pegging the man in the center of his chest with the heavy blade. He snatched it free as he dashed past the dying gunman and it seemed like for every one that Marion dispatched two popped up in its place. He silently murdered another shooter, slashing the man across the vital arteries of the neck. He used his dying breaths to scream and that alerted the other men. The volley of rounds opened up again on Marion as he ran circles around them. They start lobbying dynamite sticks but he was a step quicker than most of them. He switched tactics from stealth to full on strikes, shooting and moving; each round hitting its mark with professional precision.

Kyra lay unconscious in that hollowed tree safe from the lurkers, sleeping soundly through the mayhem. It wasn't until the barrage of ear ringing explosions thrust her back to consciousness. Her head was swimming like a school of fish which made it difficult for her to coherent.

A nearby explosion triggered her reflexes and she shielded her face from the blast. All of her memories rushed back to her and she peered out into the dark landscape looking for her father. On shaking, unsteady legs she raised up, using the tree's trunk as a brace until she could get her feet under her. Another explosion showered her with black dirt and bits of debris. A few men spotted the young girl wandering aimlessly through the forest. A shooter lit the wick of his dynamite and cocked his arm back with the intention of tossing it right at her feet. As his arm swung forward, Marion materialized and placed a shot dead center of the man's hand. The explosion was increasingly devastating as it ignited the other sticks tucked around his belt line. The shooter vanished in a fireball that lit up the forest. A stick of TNT bounced in the dirt between Marion and Kyra, with no time to think he just reacted by pouncing on top of the explosive.

He shouted for Kyra to run and take cover when the thing exploded. His body suppressed the boom, absorbing most of the blast and sparing her but he reached the extent of physical abuse his body could withstand. This last force was too great. Darkness crept around the corners of his vision and though he fought to remain conscious the struggle was futile. The last thing he saw before his vision went completely black was a man swinging the butt of his rifle at the back of his daughter's head.

Images, like a movie reel, played out in the forefront of Marion's mind. The first image was his first wife. Her smile even after all this time still comforted him. She was beautiful, young and he could recall how he felt for her. The image of her faded and was replaced with that of his latest wife Kauchee, the mother of his beautiful baby girl, who was swaddled in her arms. She smiled down on baby Kyra and then backed up at Marion. There was an explosion and the shockwave wiped away their images like dispersed smoke. Suddenly his mind was filled with modern day weapons and visions of war. Tank cannons boomed. Attack helicopters zoomed overhead, the down force from their blades scattering burning hot desert sand over him and his men entrenched behind sand dunes. Bullets whizzed past his head as he took aim at an enemy that he couldn't lock on through the optics on his rifle. He shouted orders to his men but no one moved. He looked around him and he was alone on this sand dune.

Next, he was sitting at a table in the middle of a jungle in a village with his fellow Spec Ops group. Exotic birds flew overhead adding to the sounds of the jungle. He could feel the humidity thick and sticky like a wet towel, pressing down on him. He and his teammates conversed with the elder leader of an African tribe. The chief was adorned in bright colored garments with beads, feathers and gold pieces that contrasted with his rich melanated complexion. The chief was a thin man with a soft comforting smile and a soothing voice that seemed to calm everyone around them. The women of the village provide food that Marion couldn't immediately identify and a drink that was a mixture of fruit and water. The tribe required

Marion's team's protection from a rebel faction that had been setting raids against the villagers for months, killing a handful of the citizens of the village. The tribesmen spoke broken English, so they needed a translator as their go between.

The elder said, "Strength is power but power is fleeting. Wisdom outlives youth but together as one, they are mighty tools for success. 'Elders for guidance, Young men for war'. You would do well to remember this proverb for it will assist you in time."

# Chapter 14

Darkness overtook Marion again and this time when his eyes opened, he wasn't in a humid, lush tropical environment, or the harsh theater of war in the Middle East. He was in a dark musky room. Light streamed in through wooded slacks in the roof and it smelled of farm animal dung and hay. He was in a barn. His hands were tied together above his head with rough, thick twine that bit into his wrist annoyingly and he was suspended off the ground. Shirtless and weaponless.

He assumed he was alone until he heard the sound of someone whittling behind him. He craned his neck as far behind as he could and saw a young boy intensely carving into a chunk of wood. The adolescent was preoccupied with his arts and crafts but when he finally looked up and noticed Marion was watching him, he dropped his blade and pelted through the barn doors.

Dawn approaches and the first rays of the golden sun crack the seal on the horizon, piercing the veil of darkness and casting light on the events of the night before. Numerous pairs of rubber sole gore-tex military grade steel toe boots encroach into the section of the woods that the previous evening hosted an intense conflict.

The time traveling soldiers had arrived hours after Marion and his daughter were captured and were taken hostage by Dunner's men but not before Marion had the opportunity to send dozens of Dunner's militiamen to their early graves. The air was thick with a mixed scent that lingered. It stunk of burnt copper and black powder. The team surveyed the grounds, studying the carnage that surrounded them. There was a detailed story here inscribed in the earth, one that interested them. As the team spread out, they discovered bodies, lots of them in various stages of death and decay. There were numerous charred spots dotting the perimeter. Scorched earth and trees and corpses.

S1 studied the terrain and the layout of the battlefield reconstructing a reel in his mind of what transpired. The bodies were strewn about in ¾ moon shape and he was standing in the center of it. They noticed all the bodies were white men, some law men while others just average men.

"These people were attempting to flank someone."

As S1 slowly spun around the scene unfolded in his mind. Where all the angles intersected, stood a tall, gnarled oak tree where the trunk was wide and naturally hollowed out at its base. The lead paced around the tree examining the grounds around it. He knelt down glancing inside of the tree trunk for any clues when saw a few burgundy-colored spots that stood out against the soft greens and faded shades of apricot within the tree bark. S1's onboard A.I. systems integrated into his suits fabric analyzed the organic sample after he touched it confirming it was human blood droplets.

"We got blood over here."

One of the swimmers on the other side of the semi-circle chimed in.

"Shit. Boss, you'll wanna come check this out. We got a live one over here."

The swimmers converged on that central location where they found a militiaman clinging to life. He was half slumped over resting on the broadside of a tree. The front of his shirt was burgundy, coated in a thick layer of dried sticky blood and his chest was riddled with bullets. His skin was pale as a fish's belly and his breathing was labored.

"He's fucked up pretty bad," said the operative.

"S4, check his vitals."

The swimmer followed orders and gingerly raised the downed man's wrist using his thumb to locate a pulse, it was weak but steady. The nanofibers woven into the swimmer's suits performed an array of feats displaying the critical man's physical condition from a single touch.

"He's experiencing hypotension. Blood pressure is 80 over 50 and declining. His body temperature is 95.8 degrees, also declining. He's bleeding out, sir. He doesn't have much longer."

S1 knelt down over the man who was staring death in the face. The drop in internal temperatures caused the militiaman to become delusional, muttering incoherently but S1 needed him to pull his fragmented mind together long enough to extract some kind of useful intel from him before the man expired. A few stiff slaps across the face returned some of the militia man's senses, briefly.

"Who did this to you?" At first the man's whispers were too inaudible to decipher. S1 slapped the infirmed man again and again repeating his question. The man gasped and began screaming at the top of his lungs as if the memories were suddenly reuploaded in his brain.

"The Blac....Phant....asm. The Black Phantasm ....did this...did thi........."

The sudden escalation in his heart rate pumped out the last bits of precious fluid sustaining the militiaman and the life drained from him. It wasn't the team's first time witnessing a person transition from this realm to the next, but the look of utter fear cemented on the man's face was disturbing.

"He's gone."

"Black Phantasm? A ghost or something?"

"Correct S4, but we're not here chasing ghosts. S2, see if you can find anything in the historical archives about a Black Phantasm."

S2 went to task browsing the vast wealth of historical knowledge stored on their A.I. server. It only took seconds to pull up a story pertaining to Black Phantasm folklore.

"Got something. It reads that in this area there was slave gossip about a supernatural being that rampaged up the east coast following the path to freedom town. Cutting a swath of death in its wake. No slave masters or their families survived. Slave patrollers and basically any other enemies were slaughtered as well. It goes on about arson the same as before.

The Black Phantasm transformed into a rallying call for uprisings. There was never any real evidence of an actual individual existing. The lore built up a tremendous following then just like that it seemed to vanish after a fierce battle ensued that took place at a plantation.  John Levy's tobacco farm on October 1, 1856. That's today sir! That plantation is a little over 2 clicks northwest of our current position."

"We're moving out!"

Levy's Plantation

Marion's mind raced with endless equations of how to free himself from his current predicament. The ropes binding his hands were tight enough to where it provided little wiggle room. Suspended for God knows how long, gravity's pull has begun to wear on his muscles and joints increasing fatigue.

Goosebumps coat the top layer of his skin as brisk winds blow in through the opened doors. Midday after dangling for hours, Marion finally heard the sounds of people approaching.

Two white men appeared hauling a hefty load of orange glowing embers set in a sturdy metal bucket that hissed when they placed the bucket down on the barn floor. One of the men removed a long dagger like blade from his belt line and slid the sharp end down into the glowing embers to the hilt . The two men looked up at Marion and chuckled ominously before marching back out of the barn. The bucket of burning coals was a prelude for things to come.

A while later Marion heard a collection of voices approaching, it was far more than two people this time. Then he saw Dunner, who walked in with his chest puffed up full of pride. Marion was seeing a ghost for the second time in his life. Dunner walked up to Marion and stood before him observing the myth, the legend in the living flesh as he swung helplessly. Dunner strolled around Marion and it wasn't until he returned to front and center that he spoke, sort of. Dunner planted several vicious rib shattering body blows to Marion's mid-section; the sound of a body being welled on is undeniable.

"See, that's the part that has me bewildered for a man of your stature. Impervious to damage but yet rib shots you can feel. I guess you can feel all of it though, right? Laying on a stick of TNT pushed you to your limits. That was my idea by the way, I'm pretty proud of myself if you ask me. I saw you take a bullet to the head and live."

Dunner delivered a few more vicious blows to Marion's torso and a cheap shot in his groin that made Marion vomit as Dunner erupted in laughter.

"This is too much fun, monkey. See, nothing seems to penetrate that exterior and yet somehow you still yield the same results as if you did. You truly are a special breed of nigger, aren't you? But see I…. I can appreciate your blessing. You're gonna be loads of fun."

Dunner stepped towards the bucket of blazing hot coals and pulled a wide strip of cloth from his back pocket wrapping the cloth around the hilt of the blade. He gradually removed the knife and examined its radiant orange glow. Beads of sweat immediately formed on his brow from the immense heat the blade generated. Marion knew exactly what Dunner planned to do with it next.

# Chapter 15

"I know this isn't going to yield me the reward I'm seeking but it'll do for the moment. I'm going to take my time with you, boy. This is how I see it, man that can't die, shouldn't feel pain. But then I got to thinking and realized I was going about it all wrong. You absolutely do feel pain. I just wasn't tapping into the right sources."

An evil grin blossomed on his scarred face as he snapped his fingers. Minutes later a group of men, John Levy in attendance, came in dragging Kyra by her arms.  Around her eyes were red and puffy, evident she had been crying.

Her clothes had almost been completely ripped off of her body and the piece of tattered rags clung together by threads and strands. When she saw Marion she pulled against the clutches of her captures yearning to be in the safety and protection of her father and when they wouldn't release her, she screamed. Marion trembled as waves of fury began to well up in him.

"Aww, see? That's it. There it is. The soft spot I was looking for. Now, I would never have guessed it but God has a sense of humor. First time I saw this niglet I thought to myself, 'Self, why does this little bitch seem so familiar to you?' And myself replied, 'Well it's because she is.' I mean all of you look alike but it was those eyes. I've seen them before but where? Ah yes, the last time I saw them, I watched them glaze over with death. She didn't last long which was a shame really. Who would've known almost two decades later I'd get my chance at seeing those pretty green eyes lifeless again."

Dunner hovered the sizzling blade close to Kyra's youthful face. The wet streams of tears that streaked down her cheeks instantly dried as she recoiled. Dunner rejoiced in her reaction, finding delight in the delicious fear.

"Now I just can't figure out what I want to do. Should I kill her and make you watch or kill you in front of her? Which hurts more? Decisions, decisions."

"DUNNER! Let her go! It's me you want! I'm the one that took away everything you loved. Your problem is with me, not her!"

"WRONG YOU SUMBITCH! You and your whole gotdamn kind is my gotdamn problem! All of ya! The only things you're good for is hard labor and the occasional fuck when we feel like it! You took away more than my family, my children. When you mercilessly killed them, you killed the part of my soul that could deal with even seeing you niggers walking around. When you talk it disturbs my peace. Your very breathing is an insult but you gave me a gift and for that I'll say thank you. I'm gonna peel the skin off of her pretty little self and you're gonna watch every second of it!"

Marion burst into manic laughter that took everyone including Kyra by surprise. Dunner turned toward him with confusion on his face.

"You wanna talk about gifts, huh? God gave me gifts but you know that. All of you have seen or heard about my gifts. As a spec ops warrior I was trained by my superiors on the art of death. How to kill efficiently. My sergeants told me to never take the killings personally and I never did. But your wife, your kids, I took joy in bleeding them like farmed pigs."

"Shut your got damn mouth! YOU SHUT YOU FUCKING MOUTH RIGHT NOW!"

"Your wife. The look on her face when she saw my black ass creep into your bedroom, whew. She wanted to scream, I could tell that but fear gripped her heart. She sat there and watched me as I dragged your punk ass off the bed kicking and screaming then I drove that knife through you. I apologize that you survived such an ordeal. Normally I don't miss my mark. You were supposed to die that night, but you didn't."

"SHUT YOUR FUCKING BLACK ASS MOUTH, BOY! I'M WARNING YOU!"

"She called for you. She begged for you to get up. She too cried as the blade slid across her throat. The sound it made slicing through her trachea. It was.... Satisfying."

Dunner charged Marion screaming like a banshee as he shoved the blade into Marion's abdomen. Though the sharpened edge never pierced his skin that didn't hinder Dunner's attempts as he repeatedly stabbed at him until the blade snapped in half and fell to the ground causing a small pile of hay to smoke and smolder. Then he continued stabbing with the broken side, eventually abandoning the weapon all together and opting out to use his hands to continue to pummel Marion. He punched until fat drops of sweat stained the dirt floor around him.

When he felt like his heart was about to burst Dunner stopped and pulled his pistol, firing every round in the chamber. As the revolver's chambers emptied, Dunner's sanity returned. He was heaving and what little bit of hair decorating the top of his head was disheveled. Marion's damage remained internal as his body was racked with the pain of that brutal assault but he had accomplished what he'd set out to do.

The attention had shifted from his daughter to him. The knife he threatened to use to inflict pain on Kyra was destroyed. That granted him a little more time to devise a plan. Dunner wiped the sweat from his face with the sleeve of his jacket and used his hands to style the fragile strands of blond hair back into place. Once he'd gathered himself, he holstered his pistol.

"Forgive me, years of trauma have destroyed my levels of patience to almost nil. Gentleman if you will, please cut our esteemed guest down. Restrain him and escort him to the courtyard where I have a surprise waiting. I grow weary of this monkey. He wants to be remembered as a ghost. Well so be it. Your wish is my command."

And with that Dunner bowed sinisterly as one of the men went and cut the rope anchored to the ground that held Marion suspended. His weakened joints buckled under the returned weight, and he crumpled up. Two men lashed lengths of rope around his neck on either side of him and tugged in the opposite directions restricting his airflow. Marion struggled to stay on his feet which were like pins and needles as he was dragged out into the open.

On the far end of the property the group had regathered around a large object that was obstructed by the mass of moving bodies. It wasn't until Marion was closer that he recognized what the object was. An artillery cannon set on top of a rolling platform. Dunner stood on the opposite end of the large bore weapon staring maliciously as Marion was pulled closer and closer.

# Chapter 16

From the woods the quartet of future soldiers were camouflaged under the brush of leaves and branches. They'd been camped out for hours patiently observing the Levy plantation from afar. According to the historical records, the legend of the Black Phantasm led them to this place. The group noticed movement all around the property but nothing significant and no signs of their man. S1 instructed S3 to send up a surveillance drone to provide them with an overhead view. The drone was dark gray, sleek in design about 6 inches in length with four rotary hover ports that produced near soundless propulsion. No one heard the mini mechanical object as it zipped through the skies. The drone relayed images to the soldiers' goggles in 4k digital real time. S2 and S1 were assigned long range DMR's with powerful scope that they used to sweep back and forth over the plantation.

"Boss, are you seeing this?"

Through the high powered scope, S2 spotted several white men dragging a battered looking younger black female across the yard towards the opened doors of a barn. Minutes ago prior to that another larger group of men ventured over to that same barn. There was something definitely going down in that structure but they couldn't make out what from that angle and distance. They didn't want to risk any of the locals spotting the drone. After a while they heard a series of gunshots and moments later a man with scars on his face came barreling out of the barn back across the field. He pointed to something out of view as the men ran off to retrieve whatever it was.

Then the future soldiers saw a man being drugged out of the barn, ropes tied around his neck like an animal. S3 zoomed in on the man and enhanced the imagery. It was Marion, facial recognition confirmed it. S1 swung the scope of his rifle back towards where the scarred man had gone and saw him standing behind a cannon.

Near the barn, Marion's capturers kicked him in the back of his knees causing him to kneel a few yards away from the cannon's opening. The dark hole seemed to go on infinitely inside the cannon. Dunner's nefarious grin had returned to his marred face as he looked down on him. Every time Marion tried to get to his feet one of Dunner's goons would put him back down. Marion watched as the men prepared the artillery weapon to be fired. Once the primer was set, they handed off the rope attached to the striker and then stepped to the side. Dunner must've seen the look on John Levy's face and it had to be one of nausea and sickening regret at what was about to occur. This spurned an idea in Dunner's dark deranged mind.

"Mr. Levy. Please, if you will, come stand by me good sir. You were gracious enough to facilitate the accommodations for tonight's events. It is only right and customary that you be the one given the opportunity of putting an end to this nightmare of a man."

Dunner raised the rope towards John Levy who hesitated at first but the pressure of all the other mob members and the slaves watching from afar, he knew he had to present himself as brave in their eyes. Otherwise, they would lose respect for him and therefore his business might suffer. So with a thick gulp, he swallowed his fear and took ahold of the rope. John Levy was a cruel man that whipped his slaves mercilessly but he'd never blown a man apart with a load of round shot let alone at point blank range. He worried the splattering of the man's body would permanently stain his fine white cotton suit. It was fall and the weather was mild but he was sweating profusely.

John pulled the rope taut and a millisecond before completing the motion, two things occurred simultaneously. Marion heard a familiar sound in the distance. A muffled chirping like a bird in a tunnel or the silencer of a large caliber rifle. One of the mob members stepped up shoulder to shoulder with John, guessing he wanted a better view of the coming carnage. Marion got his answer half a second later when the mob member's head violently snapped to the left as a burst of red coated John's whole right side.  The man's body fell limp like a wet handkerchief draped over the top of the cannon. Another chirp and the man standing behind John fell as well, in the same fashion. Marion knew now that it was a silenced rifle and that the second bullet was for John but he instinctively ducked right on time and missed its lethal kiss.  John, in a panic, attempted to yank the primer cord but right as he tugged on the rope a small but devastating explosion rocked the base of the cannon propelling shattered wood and fragments of iron scattering out in all directions. Marion felt the heat from the blast wash over his face as the shock wave knocked him on his back.

Minutes earlier the future soldiers were observing the gathering. There was no audio but years of combat trained those men to read lips and body language and what those men were saying was all bad. They watched as the man in the black handed off the control rope to the man in the white. Realizing what was about to happen, the future soldiers took action. S1 placed the cross hairs over the man in the white but when he pulled the trigger another man unknowingly stepped up and bit the bullet. S2 fired a follow up shot that terminated another man but the man in the white still held onto the control rope that activated the cannon.

"S3, take out the cannon."

S3 was piloting the drone via a forearm mounted control module. He switched the drone from auto pilot into manual mode and directed the drone in a dive bomb pattern towards the base of the cannon. He activated the drone's self-destruct function before it smashed into the cannon's platform. The explosion coupled with the copious amounts of black powder packed into the bore of the cannon made for a magnificent fiery display. The team had to wait a few seconds for the smoke and debris to dissipate before they could reacquire a clear image.

Marion was down but they saw movement like he was coughing as he rolled over onto his chest before pushing himself up on his hands and knees. He was ok from what they could see. The team collectively exhaled. They surveyed the others and as they expected a number of the men were incapacitated, some writhing in pain, others lay silent and motionless. The man in the white suit was recovering as well. He moved as though he were dazed and assessing what happened. The man dressed in black was already on his feet swaying but moving out of view as he towed the struggling young black girl against her will with him.

Marion pushed himself to his feet and shook the blast off, clearing the fog that threatened to creep around the edges of his vision. He spotted Dunner staggering towards the crop fields, a hand over the side of his head, his other hand gripping his daughter's wrist. He was about to give chase when he heard John Levy coughing. John was getting to his feet when he noticed the blast had destroyed the bindings holding Marion prisoner. When he looked around and saw Dunner was gone he immediately went for his pistol. He fired two shots that smashed into Marion's face and forehead causing zero damage. Marion gripped John by his shooting hand and wrenched it at an angle that caused the series of tiny bones connecting the wrist to the hand and forearm to pop like bubble wrap. The shooting pain arrested John as he screamed in agony and dropped the weapon. Marion delivered a bone crushing elbow to John's nose, a geyser of blood spurted out as he spun around and planted two body shots to either side of John's tenderized flanks that caused him to double over.

Marion dropped to one knee and sent a strike to the inside of John's left knee that ruptured the tendons and cracked the bone. A final arm bar into a hip toss landed John on his back gasping for air and Marion rolling over on top of him with his hands still clasped around John's arm. Extending the full length of his body and in one motion Marion pulled John's shoulder out of the socket with a grizzled pop. John shouted as he fell to his side.

"Please, mercy! I didn't. I wasn't gonna pull the trigger, I swear!"

Marion looked down on the broken man ready to end him and then he glanced over to the shiny pistol gleaming in the grass just feet away from them. Marion looked up from the gun at one of John's slaves who stood there unsure of what to do. Marion glanced back down at the pistol then back up at the slave again.

"It's on you. Your freedom or your captivity. The choice is yours."

Then the faint screaming of his daughter caught his attention as he dashed off in the direction that Dunner retreated. The slave's attention went from his master, the pistol and back a few times before he made the decision and scooped up the pistol, cocking the hammer back and aiming the gun at John's head. Marion heard the crack the pistol made as it was fired from behind him. Without turning back, he knew what choice the slave had made and it was the right one.

Dunner ran until his body teetered on the edge of collapse. When he stopped, they were standing in the middle of a barren tobacco field. He had his arm wrapped tight around Kyra's throat and his pistol pressed tightly to her temple. He constricted her breathing and that was evident at her weakened attempts at freeing herself, but Dunner easily overpowered her. His body tensed up when he saw Marion stalking up to them. He jerked Kyra's tiny frame side to side to settle her down.

"Black Phantasm, huh!"

Marion stretched his hands out motioning that he wasn't a threat.

"Dunner, I remember you that you lost a lot at my hands but I lost a lot at your hands too. Two wrongs don't make it right. She's all that I have left in this world. She's all that matters to me now, her safety. So, I'll make a deal with you. Release her to me unharmed and I'll let bygones be bygones. No harm, no foul. I'll take her and you'll never see me again. The killings will stop. The fires, all of it. Just let my daughter go. Please."

Dunner adjusted his grip on the pistol as he thought over Marion's words. Fury had him ready to hurt this Phantasm in a way that conventional weapons never could have.

"The man that can't be killed," Dunner said with sick laughter. "You sir have been a black ass thorn in my side for a long gotdamn time. In this world, I'm the law! I'm at the top of the food chain. Me! Your kind is supposed to live under my boot heel. Bow down to us! You killed my wife, my children. There will never be a way to settle that debt! I have the only thing you care about in life so in essence I have your life!"

Kyra's cries were louder now as she grappled with Dunner's meaty arm bearing down on

151

her windpipe. Marion lowered his eyes to hers and spoke directly to her.

"Baby girl, I've been out of your life for way too long. That's over. I'm here now, with you and I promise that everything will be ok. No one will hurt you ever again that I can promise you, baby girl."

"Oh yea?!" Dunder sneered. "Hollow promises, you shouldn't make those types of promises. You'll spend your lifetime regretting breaking them."

Marion stopped advancing on Dunner and stood still, his body becoming rigid.

"Last chance, Dunner. Let ...her.... go ...."

The tone of Marion's command offended Dunner, causing him to cock the hammer back on the pistol. The look in his eyes was determined. One of a man that has already made up his mind and has made peace with the actions he's taken and about to take.

"Last chance! You have no leverage in this and you're giving me demands, huh? Ok. Hey, little nigger bitch, look your father in his cold black eyes and tell him goodbye and that you'll see him in hell…. This nightmare ends today!"

"Baby listen, look at me. It's ok. He won't shoot you."

Dunner took that as a challenge and without a second thought pulled the trigger. The click was so loud and audible that it sent a shiver through Kyra's body. A click but no bang Kyra's tightly knit eyes slowly opened as the understanding that she wasn't dead dawned on her. It was a combination of confusion and relief. Dunner pulled the trigger again and again and again but all he received were hollow clicks. Confused as to how he wasn't grasping the corpse of a headless bloody young dead girl but a living one had him flabbergasted.

"You can't shoot anyone, if you don't have bullets in the gun…."

Dunner wore the unbridled expression of shock over his beaten brow. In the mayhem and chaos, he never recognized that he didn't reload his weapon after his momentary psychotic meltdown in the barn. It never even crossed his mind. When the unexpected attacks occurred, followed up with the explosion, he just took Marion's daughter hostage and fled to the fields. Before Dunner could react Marion had lunged forward knocking the three of them to the ground. They wrestled and Marion allowed himself to be taken on his back because he needed Dunner preoccupied with him just long enough for his daughter to scuttle away to safety. Once Marion was satisfied she was a good distance away from the fight he returned his attention to the man that was attempting to choke him out.

Marion easily overpowered the older man's grip, pulling one of Dunner's thumbs to the side causing it to slip out of the socket with no resistance. He thrusted upward with an open palm strike underneath Dunner's chin that caused his jaw to snap shut, clicking his teeth together hard enough to crack the enamel. Dunner's mouth filled with the copper tang of blood. Marion grabbed him by the collar and pulled him into a vicious head butt that sent Dunner doubling over in pain but he wasn't done with him yet. Marion rolled over, now he was on top and mercilessly rained down blows that blurred the lines between conscious and unconscious for Dunner's whose eyes fluttered indicating some degree of brain damage. Marion stood him up and buried his knee deep in Dunner's abdomen causing the man to vomit on the moist soil. As he was hunched over he had a sly thought and tried a sucker punch but Marion knew he would attempt that because he was a low life piece of shit human being. Easily he slipped the poorly structured swing and repaid the effort with a few of his own, each one chipping away at what little fight the man had left in him. A stream of blood mixed saliva poured from Dunner's ruined maw.

"You were right about one thing; the nightmare ends today."

Marion gut checked Dunner and spun him around so his back was to him then he looped his arm around the dazed man's throat and pulled down. The inconceivable pressure surmounting on the fragile upper neck vertebrae ruptured the thin cartilage cushions between the boney sections. And like dominos, the vertebrae fractured and split one after the other instantly killing him. Marion held on for one second longer than necessary ensuring he was dead before releasing his body which fell to the dirt, a death stare fixated on his face.

He kicked the body away from him then searched for his daughter who had nestled up beside some bales of hay. She had watched the entire brawl knowing that this was the only outcome. Still she has never seen a man be killed before up close in her life. She glared at the dead body in a trance until she felt the warmth of her father's hand on her cheeks redirecting her attention from the cooling corpse to his loving arms.

"It's over. It's over, baby girl. You're ok now, we're ok now."

After a few minutes they stood, still holding onto each other. Neither one actually wanting to let the other go. Kyra never felt so safe, truly safe in the 15 years of her short life until this very second. She was an adolescent, only a few years from being labeled as grown but right then and there she wept like a 2-year-old but these tears weren't tears of pain or agony. They were tears of joy. Marion pulled her in tighter. He was grateful that he had found his daughter and that she was safe. He would take her away from here and give her a fair chance at living a good life, a free life.

That's when both of them spotted four men approaching them from the other side of the field. The men looked odd to Kyra; they wore strange clothes and carried even stranger items in their hands. Marion however knew the suits well and more than likely the men approaching them. The future soldiers stayed in a loose formation as they crossed the space. All of the slaves and plantation helpers looked on as the warriors passed by them unsure if these were friends or foe. Their eerie green back lit oculus worn around their eyes and dark metallic colored suits made them look otherworldly.

"Father!"

"It's alright, baby, these are some friends of mine."

S1 disengaged the locking device that secured his eyewear to the suits nanotech function and slid the goggles up over his head. Pulling down the face mask portions revealed that S1 was a white man which made Kyra tense up. He noticed and gestured with his hand that she was ok. The smile on his face seemed genuine to her so she relaxed partially but she never let go of her father's arm. S1 and the other future soldiers looked around for a bit, amazed at the amount of chaos one man caused.

"Well, I guess we know what you would do if you had a time machine."

All five men burst out into laughter that broke the final pieces of proverbial ice that floated between them as Marion stuck out his hand and thanked the others for their help. The soldiers introduced themselves to Kyra and she did likewise even managing a modest curtsy.

"Look Marks, it took some time and effort to track you down, well not much effort. Once we came up on the story of the Black Phantasm it was pretty easy to find you. Talk about breadcrumbs." shaking his head, laughing. "Hey kid, how does it feel having a dad that's viewed as a superhero?"

"A super what !?!"

"Right, that word hasn't even been invented yet." laughter ensued throughout the group. "But look Marks, on a serious note, it's time to take you home. The Doc's probably got a million questions for you and I'm sure he's gonna want to run some tests, the whole gambit."

S1 pulled a skiff unit from a pocket on his suit and handed it off to Marion.

"Let's go, there's no telling how much damages you've caused in this century or in the future."

Marion examined the technology briefly, understanding this was his sole link back to his time period. Fast food, central heat and air, cellphones, robots, football. All the things this time period lacked. But then he saw the beauty and innocence held in his daughter's face and realized that it all meant nothing when compared to her. He could go without seeing another Raiders game or eating another burger from Five Guylaxy. What he couldn't go without was her.

"You know what soldier, I'm good."

S1 was puzzled at the response. Marion wasn't from this time period and remaining here hadn't even crossed their minds. Marion would stick out like a sore thumb and on top of that it's 1856. Things would surely get worse in this country long before they would get remotely better for people like them.

"Hey buddy, are you sure about this? I mean, this is your last ticket out of here. You know history. Things get pretty hairy for Black people really soon. If it's your daughter you're worried about, can we Chronolink her so we'll know her position, skip to the future and discuss the possibilities of bringing her into 2040? If that works for you."

"Naw, she's pure. I want to keep her that way. 2040 is 2040. Seems like much simpler times here. I appreciate the offer but I'm gonna have to decline."

Sighing, "The doctor won't be happy with this news, Marks, you know that."

Marion nodded as he wrapped an arm around his daughter again.

S1 looked back at the other soldiers then back at Marion.

"So, what's the story we're bringing back to the Doc? Maybe Marks didn't make it?"

S2 chipped in with a suggestion.

"I mean this is a wicked looking battle scene? Lots of bodies. It's believable that Marks was a casualty. Jumping the Chronostream with deceased organic material probably wouldn't make it through the journey right, Boss?"

"Right. How about you S3, S4?"

"I don't know, Boss. Was a lot of shooting. I saw the explosion then Marks was gone."

"Shit happens, Boss. People die. They'll have an amazing service for him. Probably get a medal or something. Don't worry, bro, I'll accept it on your behalf." Giving a slight bow.

S1 spoke, "I guess it's settled then. Are you sure you wanna do this? Once we jump it's gonna be impossible to locate you again. Unless you reopen the family business."

Marion chuckled at the statement knowing full well where the sentiment came from. He looked down to his daughter who was smiling at him and the other men. She had no idea what they were talking about. She just knew the feeling was joy and that's all she really cared about.

"This whole thing was because I was searching for something that I had, lost, had it again and then thought I lost it for good. But now, I know better. I'm done."

S1 looked around at the fires still blazing and the slaves revolting against the angry white mob members that still remained. The slaves cheered for a victory that was long overdue. "From the looks of it, things are just getting started. Last chance, Marks."

"Yea, I'm sure."

 S1 reattached his oculus and turned towards his men. "Sync up. Chrono jump on my mark. 3...2... See you around Marion."

"No, you won't."

 And with that the soldiers activated their skiffs. The air around them became super-heated and created loose wave patterns as the particles shifted in the atmosphere. There was the signifying plasmatic burst of energy that jettisoned a small shock wave an orb of pure light and then just like that the future soldiers were gone. Kyra was looking around at the chaos as well but she didn't see mad men on a killing spree. She saw the spirit of caged lives being set free!

"So, Poppa, what do we do now? Where to, from here?"

 Marion fixed her hair and looked around again.

"The future, baby girl. The future."

# Epilogue

Six years later would be the start of America's most impactful conflict to ever touch her shores. The start of the Civil War. A battle that literally split the country in half. Though the Confederate soldiers held the upper hand, being natives to the South and acclimated to the high heat and extreme living conditions but had it not been for the overwhelming participation of the countless black soldiers who'd volunteered on the Union's side, making up almost half of the soldiers fighting to keep the country together, the spoils of war would have certainly gone to the Confederates. It goes without saying that the majority of the freedmen making up those masses volunteering to fight were the direct result of those freed during Marion's siege. His impact on history was bigger than anyone could've ever imagined.

Present Day

The future soldiers returned to their timelines where an anxious Dr. Stansfield stood awaiting hopeful good news. The materialization of just four men yielded him his answer. The soldiers were debriefed and provided detailed statements about

163

the mission. Every soldier's story was the same; they all stated that Lt. Marion Marks had become a P.O.W. and during the rescue attempt he was unfortunately a casualty. Dr. Stansfield crossed his heart and mumbled a prayer. He was saddened by the news but also relieved. There were no loose ends to clip. Cleaning up a mess of this magnitude would be relatively easy.

Each member of the program was either reassigned to new detachments after being reminded of the concrete NDAs they had signed at the start of the mission, or they would be forced to retire from government altogether. The political officials in charge of the program were weary of the implications involved with tampering with the fabric of time and space. There was no telling what the punishment could be for endangering the whole of humanity. Before them, none had attempted this and no one was successful. They weighed their options and determined the intel was too volatile for anyone at this current time and voted to bury the whole thing, only promising to return to the project if the need ever arises. To deter future accusations or indictments they all swore an oath of secrecy. The program was disbanded and shut down. The future soldiers' Skiffs, tech, and hard drives attached to their A.I. chest rigs were analyzed and all pertinent intel stored were on secured files not even accessible by top level clearance before the hardware was wiped clean and then destroyed. It was as if Project Chronostream never existed.

Washington, DC 2045

The Lakoli Institution of Education and Research

The Lakoli Institution was the biggest museum in Washington, DC and one of the most renowned institutes for the history of Black Americans both here in the states as well as abroad. Today, the Institute hosts a series of government funded programs including school field trips to learn how Black Americans' contribution to the nation placed the United States at the top of the globe in economics, politics, and social status. Granting the nation, the esteemed privilege of awarding any and all that comes to her shores with a fair and just opportunity at the American dream and so much more.

Excited children by the dozens filed off their school buses and into the staging areas inside the Museum. This is a trip that every child has looked forward to, especially the Black ones since the museum's erection back in the early 90's. Chatty children, excited and hopped up on juice drinks require patience but the teachers regained control of their rambunctious charges and directed them into the building.

Mrs. Rebecca Seranao, a quaint, short, quirky Latina with long hair tied up in a neat bun, was the Curator but also the Museum Educator for the next group of children scheduled to tour the grounds.

"Attention guests. First off I would like to greet you in the proper way. *I Ni Sogoma*! That means 'Good morning' in Bambara, the original language of the Malian people. Lakoli is also another word of the language, it means school. A place of learning and of education and that, my dearest guests, is what you will receive today. Mali's population, like a lot of other West African countries was grossly impacted by the devastating effects of the Trans-Atlantic slave trade but you'll learn that and so much more inside these walls. If you're ready, children, let us begin.

An hour into the tour, Mrs. Serrano was escorting the class to the Civil Wars section of the facility. Here the Institute housed memorabilia from the war era, from uniforms to rifles and pistols. All which are held in glass boxes of various sizes and shapes.

166

For this area, The Institute founded books and official military orders assigned to soldiers deployed to battle and even photographs of soldiers. The group stopped at a black and white photo of an all-Black regiment. The title of the photo read 'United States Army 81st Battalion, Virginia, 1863.'

"This is one of the first Black Regiments sanctioned as an official Battalion in the United States Army via Presidential consent, Abraham Lincoln. This regiment, which consisted of over a thousand Black soldiers, was one of several Black regiments that played a key role in turning the tide of the Civil War.
It was a claim that the majority of the Black soldiers were slaves who a few years prior, had been set free by a freedom fighter known only as the Black Phantasm.  Some say the Black Phantasm was a symbol of hope, others say it was the living embodiment of all the turmoil that the slaves endured. There was never any real evidence that corroborated these claims."

The children listened intently but one's curiosity had gotten the best of him. A young boy raised his hand.

"Yes, you have a question?"

"Yes, Mrs. Serrano. We learned the names of a lot of freedom fighters that contributed to our freedom in this country. I'm familiar with most of them but the Black Phantasm, I've never heard of this one before. Was he like Denmark Vesey? Can you explain more about him?"

Just as the Curator was about to answer the young man's inquiry an older woman's voice replied from behind the group.

"Oooo. The Black Phantasm. Absolutely one of my favorite and most treasured stories."

A woman, beautiful in her golden years with perfect brown skin and light wrinkles around her eyes and mouth that quietly gave away her age. Her hair was a gorgeous display of a thick cloud of gray locks, that were coiled into a bun atop her head like a soft crown. Her eyes were jade green and though she walked with a cane, there seemed to be an air of regalness about her. Like she was royalty.

"Stories passed down from my mother's, mother's mother as a child. She witnessed the Black

Phantasm and every time she spoke about him you could feel the electricity in her voice."

One of the mothers listening to the elder speak was intrigued by what she said and came forward to introduce herself. She wanted to ask the elder more questions about this Black Phantasm.

"Hello, Madam. I'm Carla Banks and this is my son Adian," putting an arm around the boy's shoulders. "And you are?"

A woman that had been shadowing the touring group spoke up before the older woman could respond. The lady wore a nicely tailored blazer and matching suit pants, on her feet, modest but expensive heels. She was absolutely gorgeous. Young, with cocoa colored skin so smooth she looked like melting chocolate.

"Hi Mrs. Banks, I'm Lana Stevens, Deputy Secretary and Museum Director, here at Lakoli Institute. This is the esteemed Mrs. Odula K. Marks, President and CEO of Lakoli Institute. She oversees Lakoli's total operation and she's quite versed in Black American history especially the years prior to the Civil War. You're in for a real treat."

Museum staff slid a chair over to Mrs. Marks and assisted her with her seat, taking great care with the handling of Mrs. Marks. They stood beside her as she made herself comfortable and laid her cane over her lap.

"Gather around children, I want to tell you a story…"

## THE END

# About the Author

D'Angelo Tucker is a talented new author emerging from Virginia. His passion has always been the arts. From writing movie scripts, poems to drawing, just to name a few. His family comes from a military ground which he states has made him into the person he is today, and it also sets the background for his first novel.

In his free time, D'Angelo drive trucks and works security in various events to gain ideas for his next books. *Elders for Guidance, Young Men for War* is D'Angelo's first action fiction novel.

You can find more info about him and his books at Forever Inspired Publishing,
www.foreverinspiredpublishing.com